SCOURGED
SOULS

SCOURGED
SOULS
KEITH NILES CORMAN

ReadersMagnet, LLC

Book Reviews

Throughout the novel, Corman uses imagery of wounding, scarring, and incomplete healing. Georgia itself appears as an injured entity, with its landscape lastingly scarred.

—The U.S Review of Books

Corman devotes as much of the story to the sentiments of the soldier characters as he gives to those of their loved ones back home. The author broaches another rarely mentioned topic: that of the life experiences of ex-slaves freed before the war. This is a story of many possible responses to unwelcome change, the impact each response has on the life of the one who has it, and the lives of those close to him or her.

—The U.S Review of Books

A powerfully written book, author Keith Niles Corman does an excellent job of creating a short read that packs a punch. Written to highlight the personal consequences war has on families, friends, neighbors and loved ones while the soldiers are fighting on the front lines, this book showcases how even after all these centuries, war still impacts us just as hard today and the families of those brave soldiers as much as it did back then.

—Pacific Book Review

This was a powerful and well written work that everyone should read. While a fairly quick novel to read, it is completely engrossing and engaging throughout. A wonderful cast of characters within each story makes this book feel personal and real, and does an amazing job of relaying the way events like the Civil War shaped the lives of so many away from the battlefields as well.

—*Pacific Book Review*

Scourged Souls is a magnificent story of love, loss, courage, and destruction. It's beautifully and creatively written to touch the soul of the reader and bringing alive the characters and events. The author eloquently uses the language of the Civil War, yet in a way that is still relatable to those reading it more than one hundred and fifty years later.

—*Seattle Book Review*

Corman's story plays on all of our emotions. The reader is sure to feel pride for the young men who volunteer their lives for their country, love for the relationships among families and significant others, worry for when you start hearing not-so-great news in their letters to each other (even though we readers already know the outcome), and sorrow for when not everyone arrives home after playing their part in securing our country's correct stance on human slavery.

—*Tulsa Book Review*

Corman is a talented writer who should be on everyone's lists, especially those who enjoy a good war story.

—*Tulsa Book Review*

Scourged Souls is nothing short of a masterpiece.

—*Manhattan Book Review*

I would like to dedicate this book to the memory of those effected by the ravages of war. Those who have been lost, those who have loved one's lost and those that never returned in body, soul or mind, both military and civilian. To quote General William Tecumseh Sherman, "War is Hell!"

I would also like to thank my loving wife, Martha, for her support, encouragement and patience which made this book possible. Also, "Thank you" to the fine people at Kennesaw Mountain National Battlefield Park of the U.S. National Park Service for all their dedication and inspiration for the story you are about to read.

Fallen Soldier

Bravely I stand true and strong,
Rifle in my hand,
My Captain shouts, "Hold steady, men,
We must defend our land."

My youth starts to show,
As I begin to shake,
My body's soaked, my throat so dry,
My arms begin to ache,

We silently wait for them to show,
I'm in old tension's grip,
Tears in my eyes, sweat on my brow,
Don't let my courage slip,

Their dust is riding higher,
As closer they become,
My Captain shouts an order,
I slowly raise my gun,

They halt and hold position,
Fire from their barrels fly,
Feels as if attacked by hornets,
Oh God, don't let me cry,

I close my eyes and fire back,
We return a mighty shock,
Smoke fills the air, I feel a sting,
My ground begins to rock,

It's hard to breathe, I start to choke,
My back lies in the lane,
My Captain kneels and holds me up,
Will I ever see home again?

"You're hit, my son," he says to me,
As an Angel peers over his shoulder,
"Say something, son, speak to me."
"Captain, did I fall like a soldier?"

Mother's sewing as I step near,
She sobs, then holds her heart,
Leaning down I kiss her sweet head,
But sadly I must depart.

Pa at the plow, pulls up the horse,
Then starts to stare ahead,
Must be the sun, he does that some,
His face shows signs of dread.

I cross the field this spring day,
Hugging close, whispering in his ear,
Courage, dear Father, there's nothing to dread,
Your brave Soldier Boy is here.

Peace in my heart, I gaze about,
Angels' choir in celestial song,
I bravely enter in strong and true,
To the legion I'm proud to belong.

Contents

Chapter One

FRESH SQUIRREL STEW

Will crouched in the dirt and wondered how long he would have to sit there before he could get up and stretch his legs. Next to him, Sam stirred and stepped forward, breaking a branch under the toe of his boot. Will looked at him and slapped his shoulder, silently.

"You gotta be quiet," he whispered, his words barely more than air between them.

"I know," Sam replied, in similar tone. Will wasn't impressed, and held his finger in front his mouth to drive the point home before turning back to the woods in front of them.

Both boys went back to staring hard into the trees, watching the leaves rock back and forth in the chilly air. Their patience and sore muscles paid off when they watched a fat-bellied gray squirrel poke its head out from a far branch. He looked around, his paws pulled up to his face like he was considering his options. Will watched him slowly as he pulled his musket from its place at his side and steadied it against his body.

The time of year was perfect for squirrel hunting. The summer had faded like a memory, leaving behind the cooler temperatures and falling leaves. Soon enough, winter would fall over the mountain and life would slow down until summer. It was an intrinsic need, to prepare for winter, and the squirrels on the mountain felt it the same way Will and Sam and their families did.

The squirrels were busy canvassing the mountain side for nuts and seeds to cache away for spring. They were at their fattest, packing on weight to keep them warm. Will liked to think they were also slower in the fall, burdened by both the extra fat and the exhaustion of running around the forest, and used it to his advantage.

He held the musket steady while Sam watched by his side. The squirrel had climbed farther out onto the branch and was now staring right at the boys. Will forgot the strain in his muscles as he watched the squirrel in his sight. He was ready.

The crack of the musket sounded like thunder and echoed through the woods, sending birds scattering from the treetops. The squirrel jumped and hung in the air for a second before tumbling, head over tail, through the branches and into a pile of leaves at the foot of the tree. The force of the shot knocked Will over, straight onto his back in his own pile of leaves, the gun abandoned once more at his side.

"Ya got him," Sam said, rising and staring down at his friend.

"'Course I did," Will replied. He stayed where he was a moment and watched the blue sky through the leaves. He pulled himself up and looked his gun over.

"That was the loudest yet," Sam said.

"It was. Let's get the squirrel. I bet we can bag a few more before headin' over to the Lacy," he said, starting out from the bushes they had been hiding behind and walking to the tree to claim his prize.

The squirrel was staring up at the sky, much like he had been before. Will kicked the leaves and lifted the squirrel's body before slinging it into the sack that Sam was holding. The boys trekked on through the woods, letting the leaves crunch beneath their feet as they looked for more squirrels. The squirrels may be their fattest, but the days were also shorter, and the boys had much ground to cover.

As the sun hung low in the sky, Will Braunhoff and Sam Tillet emerged from the woods on the side of the road. The mountain rose behind them as they set off in the direction of the Lacy Hotel at Big Shanty. Sam swung the bag of animals over his shoulder, while Will carried the musket and supplies.

"Got a sack full of Yankees," Sam said, swinging it.

"Watch your mouth, or your Ma will tan your hide like one of your Yankee squirrels," Will chastised him as they headed in the direction of the hotel.

The dirt road was wide and ran from Marietta to Big Shanty. The Lacy Hotel at Big Shanty was a stopover for the many folk that traveled on the "State Road," as everyone called the Western & Atlantic Railroad. Most of them worked for the railways, and they all appreciated Mrs. Lacy's cooking and hospitality. And she always appreciated Will and Sam showing up with fresh meat for her to make use of. Squirrel stew with dumplings would warm many of hearts and be an added appreciation to the menu.

The boys had grown up together at the foot of Kennesaw Mountain, in Georgia. They were almost a year apart—"ten months!" Sam would always proclaim with indignation when people rounded it to a full year. Their fathers had moved to Georgia from Ohio, having made their lives before in Cincinnati. When Will's father decided that he didn't want to work for a soap company, the men decided to make a new start.

Once they had settled in Georgia, the elder Braunhoff and Tillet married women who had grown up in the rolling mountains of the south. They erected a general store on the Marietta-Cassville road and began to sell goods to the same people who passed through and stopped at the Lacy Hotel. There were challenges, but the men were making their own future and not living for someone else. They got involved in the church and the community and soon were the familiar faces that everyone knew around town.

The boys jumped off the road and started to follow the train tracks that ran parallel to it. They could feel the ground begin to shake beneath their feet as a train approached. They scurried up the hill to a plateau where they could watch the train and not risk getting hit as it barreled by. As the heavy locomotive rolled into view, Sam saw that Pete Wilson was at the helm.

"It's Pete and the Texas!" Sam said.

"Who'd you think it'd be?" Will asked.

Sam started waving, momentarily setting his sack in the dirt at his feet. He inched closer down the side of the slope and waved some more, trying to get Pete's attention.

"Be careful," Will said. That ten-month difference was a big one when it came to making sure Sam didn't get killed by a train coming through. He kept waving.

Finally, Pete noticed Sam and waved back. The train was fast, but Pete expertly put it in reverse, bringing the giant iron locomotive to a stop at the base of the hill below where Sam stood. He raced down to get closer as Pete stuck his head out.

"What's this? Train thieves again?" he called out.

"Nah. Need a ride down to the Lacy. Can we git one from ya?" Sam hollered back. "I could manage that. But it'll cost ya a squirrel," Pete replied, pointing to the sack on the ground.

"Cheaper than a ticket," Will said, nodding.

The boys picked up their haul and skidded down to the train, pulling themselves aboard and settling next to Pete. It was Sam's dream to be an engineer, taking his own locomotive north and south across the country, carrying freight and passengers where they needed to go. He knew it was a hard, tiring job, and to get to be an engineer, one had to put in his time as an assistant. Sam didn't mind the thought of having to feed wood chunks into the firebox for a few years before making a name for himself, but his mother had other thoughts.

She wanted her son to grow up and become a man of faith—a Methodist preacher like the one in town that lead the congregation each Sunday. She didn't want her son traveling far and wide on a dangerous train without companionship, or God. Sam tried to please his mother, but knew that it would take heaven and earth to get him to go into preaching instead of riding the rails.

The Texas lumbered down the track, picking up speed as it moved past the mountain heading north. Sam watched Pete's every move while Will looked into the sack and counted the catch again.

"Best day of the season, I reckon," he said.

"Yeah, the damn Yankee squirrels didn't know what took them," Sam said, momentarily taking his eyes from the track to look at his friend.

"You're gonna slip up in front of your Ma. She's gonna take away the spendin' money you're about to get."

The train rounded the last bend and the Lacy Hotel rose up from the horizon in front of them. Pete slowed the locomotive down as they got closer, bringing it to a slower stop than the previous one. Sam picked up the sack and once again swung it over his shoulder.

"Here we are. The great Lacy Hotel at Big Shanty. Best stop on the line," Pete said, gesturing with his hand, and waving it in the direction of the hotel, as the boys climbed down.

"Thanks, Pete," Sam said.

Pete nodded, spitting a short stream of tobacco juice out the cab window, as he began to bring the train back to life. They stood next to the track and watched the monster trundle along, each car pulling the one behind it. When it was just a speck in the distance and the ground had stopped rumbling, they headed up the path to the hotel.

They bypassed the front door and went around the white clapboard building to the back kitchen, where Mrs. Lacy would be working with the staff to prepare the meal for the night. The door was closed, but the smell of pork came wafting through the windows. Will realized he was starving. Hunting took a lot out of them.

Sam bounded up the stairs and knocked on the door, resting the squirrels next to him. The door was opened by one of the kitchen hands—a girl with dark hair and blue eyes that Sam had always liked. She greeted them and invited them inside before going off to find Mrs. Lacy.

The kitchen was hot, like the summer days that were on the edge of the memory. A woman stood at the stove, stirring a big stock pot that rested on top of it. She paid no attention to the boys' presence, used to seeing them come and go with their haul.

A moment later and Mrs. Lacy came into the room, her skirt brushing the floor as she walked. She was a short woman with a round frame and kind eyes. The travelers who took refuge at the hotel, be it for the night or for a meal, always felt comfortable around her. She was the kind of person who took kindly to every stranger and was constantly offering to help out those in need.

"Hello, boys. Gettin' close to supper time. Your mothers must want you back soon," she said, tousling Sam's hair. He hated that, feeling as though it were an affection better suited for a younger boy. He minded his manners and let her continue.

"They will, for sure. But we've been on the mountain and thought we'd bring our catch down and do some business," Will said, pointing to the bag.

"Ah, I can always count on you boys to bring me something nice," she said, looking over the animals they brought.

"Yankee vermin, every one," Sam said.

"I can see that. Fancy yourself a soldier, do ya?" she asked.

"Hunters, at least. The mountain has been full of fat ones this year," Will said. "What would I do without y'all to do the tough work?"

Sam laid out the squirrels she was going to take, leaving a few in the bag for them to bring home to their parents. Mrs. Lacy wiped her hands on the starched apron she wore and went searching for a few coins to give the boys. The girl who had been washing dishes came over and took the squirrels, getting ready to prepare them.

"Well, you still have the best prices for Yankee vermin around," she said, counting the coins into Sam's hand.

"Ain't nobody can hunt like we can either. Will is a sure shot with his musket," Sam said, taking the coins and tucking them into his pocket.

"Indeed. Let me give you something for the road, you must be starvin'," she laughed as she broke off a piece of bread and handed it to each boy. They ate it quickly. "Get home to supper now, before your mothers come callin'."

The boys nodded, their mouths full of bread, before turning to the door and leaving. They jumped down the three stairs and landed in the grass, the bag landing with them. Sam picked it up and Will gathered his musket from where he had leaned it against the porch. They set off across the field that ran behind the Lacy Hotel and headed toward their homes, laughing all the way.

OBADIAH LOOKED OUT THE FRONT OF his blacksmith shop and watched his son coming down the road. Isaiah stopped, and his father watched as the Braunhoff and Tillet boys came careening down the hill to his son. They stood in the center of the road, miming hunting and fighting. Isaiah laughed. Obadiah turned from the window and went back to his work.

There was always work to be done at the shop, and Obadiah was happy for it. A free man, he didn't mind if the days were long now that he worked for himself. Born a slave, Obadiah had ended up living on the plantation of a kinder master than some. He had worked as a smith on the side, when his work was done, and the man who owned him let him as long as it didn't affect the work. Finally, his master offered him his freedom for a price. Obadiah bought his freedom and immediately set to earn enough to buy his family.

Blacksmithing was the one thing he was excellent at, and once his family had been bought, he set up his own shop near the Braunhoff General Store. People from all around came to him to have work done, and he had earned the respect of the locals. Isaiah had fallen in with Will and Sam and they often conspired on pranks and shenanigans.

Not everyone in town was keen to have Obadiah there, and his shop had been victim of raids looking for ports on the Underground Railroad. It was assumed by some of Obadiah's past as a slave made him the prime connection in the area for others looking for freedom. Obadiah had learned to patiently answer the questions that came, and offered his shop to search if needed. Obadiah's freedom had been worth more than the potential punishment that would come with smuggling other slaves to the north.

Isaiah came bounding in the door at the moment, closing it behind him. He was out of breath from running down the street.

"Hi, Pa," he said, breathless.

"Isaiah, my son. You are out of breath," Obadiah said, hanging up the heavy apron he wore while working.

"Runnin', sir," he said.

"Well, let's run to the house. I'm sure your ma has supper on the table, and your sisters are probably getting' fidgety waitin' for us," Obadiah said.

His son nodded. An orange sun hung low in the west, casting long dark shadows as the pair walked home, the dust from the red Georgia clay kicking up covering them with fine powder.

Chapter Two

ASPIRATIONS

There was no better place to live than Illinois, Elizabeth, or Nell as she liked to be called, thought to herself as she sat on the porch and watched the breeze blow the leaves in the trees. In her lap, her cross stitch sat abandoned. She was enjoying the quiet too much, and her mind kept wandering.

"Nell, I could use you in the kitchen," her mother called out through the open window.

"Of course, Mama," Nell replied, rising from the wooden bench that lined the porch. She wrapped up her threads and frame and took another look at the blue sky.

"Your father will be home soon for dinner. I believe Robert is coming with him," her mother continued.

"Yes, Father said he would be coming along this afternoon," she said as she stepped over the threshold into the cool foyer of the family home.

Nell smiled to herself as she made her way to the kitchen. She was looking forward to seeing Robert, and was glad that he was coming over for the midday meal. They were engaged to be wed, and Nell's heart soared any time she thought of the occasion, or how happy their life would be once they were husband and wife.

"Thinking about Robert again, are you?" her mother asked when she saw the look in her eyes.

"I'm not always thinking about him, you know," her daughter replied.

"No, but you are most of the time," her mother handed her an apron from the hook by the door.

The Wilkersons lived in a nice house in the center of town. It had been one of the first buildings erected, and it had been done so with a flourish. Elizabeth and her brother, Kenneth had grown up in the big halls and open rooms, hiding in cupboards and closets as children when they played.

Family life was important to the Wilkersons, and Nell and her brother were close with their parents. Her mother spent her days between taking care of the family and spending time with her church group. They were always gathering for prayer or to help those in the community. Nell was used to finding her mother in the parlor with the ladies, drinking tea and talking about the Bible.

Her father was an attorney who was well known around town. He was so good that he was occasionally called to the bigger cities to try cases. Everyone in town knew of him, and looked to him for advice around all sorts of matters—from family to business. Her father had taken a particular liking to young Robert Orberson, Nell's fiancé, and brought him on to read law under him. Nell had liked him from the first time they had met, but it was nearly a year before a marriage proposal surfaced.

When he wasn't trying law, Mr. Wilkerson worked closely with the church in town. He sat on a number of committees and helped advise the Reverend on matters in the community. He was also the leader of the Republican Committee in town, holding meetings in the church on Wednesday nights. On Fridays, the men would come over and convene in the parlor of the house, talking business and smoking cigars.

Nell and her mother moved about the kitchen with the ease of women who knew what they were doing. Her mother had a pot of soup on the stove, reheating from the day before. Nell took out a loaf of bread and sliced into thick hunks, letting the knife come down with force on the wooden butcher block. Before her brother had left, he would have passed through the kitchen at some point and stolen a piece, talking about how much he needed to be a growing man.

"I wonder how Kenny is doing," Nell said, looking at the table and the place that he normally occupied at family meals.

"Oh, he's fine. We got that letter from him last week. You read it. It sounded like he was on some grand adventure," her mother said, shaking her head.

"He always makes it sound like an adventure. He's like that. Too brave for his own good, sometimes," Nell said. She put the bread on a plate and set it in the middle of the table.

"He's like your father. The Wilkerson men have always been about bravado. But they're good men. They do the right thing. Even your brother."

"I know. Robert is a good man too. He's so brave," Nell said. She had the faraway look of a day dream in her eyes. At sixteen, being engaged to such a successful young man was a dream come true. The other girls in town were jealous that she was lucky enough to catch his eye, and that her parents approved.

"Of course he is. Your father would never approve, otherwise. He wouldn't even let him work for him if he didn't trust that he was of the strongest moral stock and character. He will make a good husband for you," her mother nodded, "you'll have to daydream less, you know."

Nell looked at her mother and saw the familiar teasing smile in her eyes. They were close, and Nell looked up to her mother as the ideal image of a wife and mother. She wanted to have her own kitchen someday, and looked forward to cooking and caring for a family of her own. She wanted more children than her parents though. She dreamed of a house full of little girls, and a wide lawn where they could hold picnics in the summer. She pictured Robert coming home from work at the end of the day and greeting her in the kitchen.

The familiar sound of the front door opening and closing caused the women to look up from their work. Mr. Wilkerson appeared in the doorway, his broad shoulders almost filling the space. He stepped into the kitchen and removed his hat, setting it on the sideboard.

Robert was right behind him, a smile on his face. Nell noticed the faint fuzz of a beard on the chin that was normally bare and she smiled. He looked so handsome in his suit and tie, his hair combed back neatly.

"Good day," Robert said, bowing slightly at the women.

"Hello, Robert, how are you?" Mrs. Wilkerson asked as she turned to her husband and gave him a kiss on the cheek.

"Very fine, Ma'am, and yourself?"

"I am good. We're glad that you two are home for lunch. Nell and I have been working up a sweat in the kitchen."

"Well, thank you for having me. I always look forward to the invitation," he said.

"Son, you barely need an invitation. You are going to be marrying my daughter. You're family. And not a terrible law clerk, either," her father smiled at Robert as he took his seat at the head of the table.

The table was long and made of pine boards. It was less fancy than the one in the formal dining room, but worked for lunches and the casual visitors. Nell carried over a pitcher of water and poured some in each glass, starting with her father's. Robert watched her, still standing in the doorway, enjoying the calm grace she had about her.

Nell turned and caught him looking at her. She felt herself blush as she tried to hide it. Robert was so handsome, and kind, and she felt herself lucky to be betrothed to him. He crossed the kitchen and took a seat across from her, his back to the wide window that looked out over the yard. Soon they were all sitting around the table.

"This smells wonderful, Mrs. Wilkerson," Robert said as he looked over his bowl of soup.

"Why, thank you, Robert. Would you like to lead us in Grace?" she asked. "Oh, please do!" Nell exclaimed, "I love listening to you when you lead the prayer."

"I would be honored," he said.

The family bowed their heads around the table and listened to Robert's deep voice as he prayed. Nell found herself getting lost in the sound of his voice, and thinking about how he would look presiding over grace at their own family table, once they were married. He paused after giving thanks and prayed that Kenneth was protected while off fighting. Nell looked up and smiled at him.

Kenneth had always been brave, and had fancied himself a soldier since he was barely able to crawl. Two years older than Nell, she had always looked up to him. They had grown up playing different games in the yard that required Ken to pretend to be a gallant fighter—perhaps a revolutionary hero, and he had never shaken the desire.

When the war started, there was a lot of talk in the town. Nell remembered how it overshadowed the conversation everywhere—from church to the dinner table. Her father was a staunch abolitionist, as were most of his friends at the law firm. She remembered how Kenneth had inserted himself in every conversation between the men—he seemed to acquire a certain swagger any time the war came up.

Nobody was surprised when he enlisted with the Union. Their mother cried into her tea in the parlor the afternoon he came back and told them. Nell cried too, but later and alone, not wanting her brother to know she was scared. He was so happy when he came home. He told their father over dinner that he had enlisted with the Iron Brigade. He had been proud; she had seen it in his eyes. Kenneth was invited to have a drink with their father after dinner, alone. He had been beaming with joy as Nell and her mother cleared the dishes.

The house had seemed so empty after he left. For the first week, their mother barely left the parlor, where she sat staring out the window. Nell had brought her tea and cookies and tried to cheer her up, but it was hard as she worried about her oldest son. Nell's father had been proud, and bragged about his son clear across town, until it seemed like there wasn't anybody who hadn't heard of Kenny Wilkerson signing up with the Union and the "Iron Brigade."

Her mother had felt better once the first letters came in, and she could tell her father did too. They both read them by the fire at night. The first few days after he left felt like a vacation—no one was teasing her or butting into her personal affairs. The truth of the matter was that she missed her brother terribly. They had always been close, and the house seemed so much quieter after he left.

Her mother checked the post every day for word, and she listened to the conversation that traveled around the sewing circle. The Iron Brigade quickly earned a reputation for being quick witted and brutal in combat, but they weren't without their losses. Occasionally, Kenneth's letters sounded like he was homesick, but he was always quick to end with a note or story about one brave act or another. Sometimes, Nell caught her mother reading them in the corner of the parlor, with quiet tears falling on her cheeks.

Months after Kenneth had left for the war, it became apparent that more troops were going to be needed. Nell's father, the brave and assertive leader that he was, immediately stepped up to fill the void and lead a group of troops to the front line. The day he made the announcement over breakfast, his wife had looked distraught. Nell remembered the feeling of worrying that both her father and brother would be on the front lines. It had, gradually, subsided.

"How is today going?" Nell's mother asked, looking at her husband. He swallowed the bite of food he had before speaking.

"Excellent. It's been an easy day at the firm. Showing Robert how he can be a little more efficient in handling briefs. This afternoon we had a drill on the field," he took a bite of soup.

As the war had ramped up, and a bigger need was had for troops, Mr. Wilkerson had stepped up to form a militia. It was comprised mostly of the younger men that had worked for her father or knew him through the church. They met and ran drills on the parade field that flanked the south side of town. Sometimes the women would gather with tea and biscuits and watch the men march back and forth across the field. Nell's mother was so proud, talking about her husband at every church meeting.

Nell was proud, too. Her father had chosen Robert as his lieutenant, a title that he wore proudly, and a responsibility he took seriously. There were moments, at night, where she worried about him facing battle. She steeled herself against such dark thoughts and instead tried to think of how handsome he was in his uniform. She and her mother would sometimes spend the late afternoon sitting in the chairs on the porch and talking about how brave they both were.

Nell had been surprised the night that Robert was announced as lieutenant in the volunteer regiment. Her father had thrown a dinner for the elite in town once he decided to lead the volunteers. He had patted Robert on the shoulder as he announced it to the table before the start of the meal. Nell had never been more proud or happy in her life, even though she was sad about him going to war and would have been happier for him to have stayed home with her.

"I am really learning a lot from your father, Nell," Robert said, looking at her with loving eyes.

"Of course you are, he's such a brave man," she smiled. Her mother patted her knee and smiled too.

"You are too kind, Elizabeth," her father said.

They ate their soup, reaching for slices of fresh bread as they worked through the bowl. Nell's mother got up halfway through the meal to prepare a pound cake for dessert, which she served on one of her nicest platters.

After lunch, her parents went for a walk around the property. Nell set about cleaning the kitchen. Robert watched her from his seat the table. Nell looked up from the dishes and smiled at him from time to time. At one point he got up and stood right next to her—so close that Nell got goosebumps.

When Mr. Wilkerson returned from his walk, Robert immediately stiffened, ready for work. After kissing his wife goodbye, Nell's father hugged her and headed for the door. Robert smiled and said goodbye to Nell before following her father out the door and back to the law office.

Chapter Three

LEAVING THE FARM

Auggie Greive swung his legs over the side of his bed and reached for the trousers that hung from the chair next to him. He rubbed his eyes and took a deep breath. Slowly, he rose and pulled the trousers on, fastening them as he yawned. He walked to the window and looked outside.

The morning's sun rose slowly over the hills and lit up the fields that rolled from the farm house out to the tree line. Auggie rose with the sun to help his father with the morning chores, and took pleasure in watching the day rise. He could hear his father's footsteps below the floor, moving about in the kitchen. He knew his mother would be rising too, and waking his younger brothers.

Tacked to the wall of his bedroom, next to the small window from which he watched the sun each morning, hung a clipping from a local paper. It detailed the Union's fearless charge into battle, and Auggie read it with pride as often as he watched the sunrise. He thought the soldiers were so brave to go off to war, and imagined what it must be like to go into battle. He admired General Grant for his leadership qualities, but longed to serve under General William Tecumseh Sherman because of his courage and tenacity.

Downstairs, his mother was setting the bowls on the table next to a pot of oatmeal from the stove. His little brothers came wandering in from their bed, rubbing their eyes with sleep.

"Mornin'," he said to them, pulling out chairs.

"Mornin'," his smallest brother, Jonas, said with a sleepy grin. He dove into his oatmeal with abandon.

"Slow down! You haven't been starved!" Mrs. Greive said with a laugh as she watched her youngest son.

Mrs. Greive was a pleasant woman with bright eyes and hair that had gone grey some time ago, though it didn't detract from her natural prettiness. She was a doting mother and a loving wife, and understood the needs of farm life.

Auggie's parents had moved to America from the Middle Rhineland over twenty years before. Back home, they had owned a small farm and worked the land. They were a peaceful family, and the farm had brought them contentment. The violent social upheaval and unstable politics in Germany and across Europe had begun to impact their ability to make a living, creating a realization that they needed to find a new home.

Settling in Indiana had been like finding a second home. Many people from the old country had come over in the years before they had, and Emmitt's Crossing had become a quiet German enclave in Southern Indiana. Suited with shared culture and values, the people of Emmitt's Crossing were content to work the land and invest in their community, finding it a comfort to be around people from home.

When the winds in their new country began to shift toward war, the Greives stayed away from getting involved. Most of the town felt the same way. After immigrating to a new home, they did not want to find their lives thrown off by more conflict and death. Auggie's parents would talk about the news late at night, on the front porch of the house that Mr. Greive had built years before. Auggie would sit against the wall under his bedroom window and listen to the bits of conversation that would roll up from where his parents sat below.

Auggie had been born on the farm, and knew nothing of the country that his parents seemed to both love and detest. He knew a little German from living in a town with so many transplants, and from listening to his parents when they slipped into their own language. He knew his parents didn't want anything to do with the war—his mother didn't like the thought of violence, and they both hated politics.

The only political cause that they could support was that of Governor Morton. They appreciated that there was someone who wanted to look out for the needs and concerns of the citizens of Indiana. Theirs was a unique state, situated in the middle of the country and myriad different opinions on the conflict. Governor Morton was a straight shooter and more than anything, he was pro-Indiana, as well as pro-Union.

"Was there any news when you were in town yesterday, Papa?" Auggie asked, buttering a biscuit and taking a bite. Crumbs fell from his mouth and his mother sighed.

"News?" his father asked, as though he didn't know what his son was speaking of.

"Yeah, of the war. What is the Union doing?" Auggie explained.

"Fighting and killing, Auggie, that's what they're doing. That's what anyone in war is doing," his father said.

The younger boys looked up with wide eyes.

"Sometimes you have to do drastic things for a cause," he countered, looking at his father.

"Sometimes. But not us, and not this time. Your mother and I came here to peacefully raise our boys."

"And not send them off," his mother added, her voice soft, but firm. "It's worthwhile!"

"So is finishing breakfast so that we can get out to the barn," his father said, taking a sip from the mug of hot, black coffee that he had.

Auggie didn't say anything else. He took another bite of his biscuit and listened to his brothers talking across the table. He didn't understand why his parents were so stubborn and hardheaded when it came to the war. He thought that they ought to be more understanding, having left a country for a new life.

After breakfast he followed his father out to the barn. The sun had broken over the tree line and the fields were bathed in soft orange light. He understood why his parents had settled here—it was peaceful and serene in the crisp morning air, accented by the soft cooing of a rain crow in the distance. The land gave them everything they needed to live, and it was a beautiful place to call home. Auggie sighed as he thought about how badly he wanted to do what he could to protect the calm and serenity that Indiana had. He reasoned that sometimes there was such a thing as necessary conflict, and this war seemed like an example.

The animals in the barn were happy to see Auggie. He reached over the low wooden pen and gave the hog a pat on the head. The animal snorted and Auggie grinned. If he became a soldier, he'd miss the farm life. But there was so much adventure.

"The cows won't milk themselves, I'm afraid," his father's voice broke through his thought.

"I'm coming," Auggie said.

"You're distracted today. I hope you're not thinkin' too much about the war. You have no cause to worry about it. The war will stay far away. Gov'nor Morton does a good job."

"I'm not distracted. Just thinking about doing the right thing. And bravery," Auggie replied.

"Sometimes being brave means staying put."

"And sometimes, it doesn't," Auggie said quietly, hoping his father wouldn't hear.

His father had heard, and was giving him a hard look. He said nothing.

"The cows," his father nodded in the direction of the milking stools.

When they were done in the barn, the sun was high in the sky. Auggie's father set off in the direction of the house to wash up. He was supposed to go into town in the afternoon. Auggie set off in the opposite direction, trekking down the hill behind the barn to the trees that lined the space between their farm and the next. Once in the woods, he wandered deeper until he came to the creek that rolled through the land. He sat on the wide rock next to it and watched the water. It seemed to sing a soothing sonnet as it playfully cascaded over the moss covered stones. Behind him he could hear the whistle of a steam locomotive echoing through his beloved Hoosier hills.

He was distracted, of course. While he and his parents had discussed the war often, he was having a hard time shaking his position on the matter. He had been up the last few nights, staring at the ceiling and wondering what he was going to do, and how he might tell his parents once he had decided.

The woods were quiet and it was nice to be able to think without the bustle of the farm and family to distract him.

AUGGIE RETURNED TO THE HOUSE AFTER his father had left for town. The house was quiet. "Where are the boys?" he asked his mother, who was sitting by the window sewing socks.

"They went with your father into town. Bless him, they will run him ragged," she said.

"They're good with him. He keeps them in line," Auggie nodded with assurance. He went back into his bedroom and once again studied the newspaper piece on the Union. The text was already fading from being displayed, and handled.

Auggie knew the words by heart, though, and found himself even dreaming about them. He took a long look at himself in the mirror.

His hair was blonde and trimmed neatly. His long nose was his mother's, and his eyes were his father's familiar blue. He was a handsome young man, as his mother was quick to tell him. He didn't care about being handsome today, focusing on the look in his eyes. He was searching to measure how much resolve he had. After all, the Union boys were willing to fight for their beliefs. He simply argued over the kitchen table.

That night, Auggie sat at the table long after it was cleared. His father noticed and sat across from him. For a while, neither of them spoke. Mrs. Greive moved around the house, handling the sleepy boys and tucking them in.

"What's on your mind, son?" his father asked, finally.

Auggie took a deep breath. "I am going to enlist," he said. The words came out almost in slow motion, and he realized he was whispering. He didn't need to repeat himself; his father had heard every word. "No, I don't think so," he said, simply.

There was another long pause as they sized each other up. In a way, both men had known that this conversation was on the horizon.

"Papa, I've been thinking about this hard. It's something that I have to do. Just like you and Ma had to leave Germany to come here," he said with a tone of confidence.

"Moving and enlisting in a war are two different things, son," his father countered, "and we came here so that you and your brothers could have an easier way of it. Not to send you off to fight."

"I know, Papa. But this is my country. I was born here. It's ungrateful to stay still and not do something."

Auggie's mother listened as she came back into the room from saying goodnight to the boys. She crossed through the room and went into the parlor, not wanting to watch her son fight to go enlist.

"You may believe it is the right thing to do, but you are not ungrateful for staying put. Plus, we need your hands on the farm. You have responsibility here."

"And what about responsibility to my country? What about keeping Indiana as peaceful as it is right now? Remember Morgan and his marauding band of rebels came close to here not so long ago? I can't sit back and let that happen again, Papa!" Auggie looked at his father and saw that he could tell how passionate his son was.

"I understand how seriously you feel—" his father began.

"Then you'll understand that I am enlisting, and that there's nothing you can do about it," Auggie said. He rose from his chair and pushed it in before his father could say anything.

His father stayed quiet and remained seated. Auggie went to the staircase that led to the small bedroom upstairs. He paused at the bottom and watched his mother join his father at the table. He realized how old they were as he stood there. They didn't say anything, and so he went upstairs with his convictions.

The next morning, Auggie was unsure of what to expect at breakfast. When he went downstairs he was greeted with a big hug from his mother. She felt sad, as though she was trying to hold him forever. The boys were quiet at breakfast, casting eyes around the table with uncertainty. They had heard most of the conversation the night before, and part of their parents' after Auggie had gone to bed.

Auggie got a bowl of oatmeal and a roll and sat at his place. He ate intently, looking into his bowl and trying not to make eye contact with his mother. When he heard his father walk into the room, he looked up.

"Good mornin'," he said.

"Mornin', son," his father replied, sitting at the head of the table, without eating and looking him over. "Listen, I've been thinking about our conversation last night. And I realize that the truth is you are mostly a man and I can't stop you from making choices that you believe are right. I can advise you to stay here, but I can't keep you," he said.

Auggie tried not to show his joy at what his father was saying, seeing how much it bothered his mother. She looked like she was on the verge of crying already. The boys stared at their father. No one said anything for what seemed like a lifetime.

"Thank you, sir," Auggie finally said, nodding his head resolutely. He felt a certain steel enter his soul as he thought about going into town to enlist.

THE SUN WAS BRIGHT ON THE day Auggie prepared to set off to Camp Dennison. Camp Dennison was located in Ohio just east of

Cincinnati, and many of the folks from the area that had chosen to enlist were ending up there. It was home to the 52nd Ohio, which would be Auggie's regiment. He would be around a lot of people who had similar German backgrounds, and he was sure he would know someone.

That morning, his mother had prepared a massive breakfast of eggs, fresh ham, hominy, redeye gravy, hot biscuits with butter, buttermilk and steaming coffee. Afterwards, the family had loaded into the wagon and headed into town. The Ohio and Mississippi depot sat at the far edge of town, the rickety wooden platform filled today with people leaving for Ohio, and their families. Auggie's brothers had been quiet all day, and his mother was fighting tears. His father had turned out to be incredibly supportive once he had enlisted, even telling him that he was proud.

He held his ticket in his hand and let his sack rest by his feet. His mother was hovering, constantly reaching out to stroke his hair like he was a small child.

"You need to stay safe. And come home to me," she said, looking at him in the eyes.

"I will, Ma. I'm not going away forever. Just goin' away to win," he smiled.

His mother held him tighter.

"You're going to squeeze the life out of him and you're worried about the war," his father said.

"I love you," she said, tears beginning to show themselves at the edge of her eyelids.

"I love you, Ma," Auggie said, hugging her tightly. He felt his heart skip when he thought about leaving, but pushed the feeling aside.

The train lumbered down the track, and Auggie and his family stood on the platform watching it approach. It roared into the station and slowed to a stop, steam rising into the air. The platform was suddenly a flurry of action—families saying goodbye, and people gathering their bags. Auggie's mother hugged him again, inhaling the smell of his clean hair one last time.

Auggie shook his father's hand.

"Be safe, son. I'm proud of you," his father said. He pulled his son into a quick hug.

"I will, sir," Auggie said.

He hugged his brothers and told them to take care of Ma while he was away. People were starting to board the train, stepping up with the help of the porters. He gathered his duffel and slung it over his shoulder before turning to the train. As he climbed the stairs, he stopped and looked back to give his family one last wave before disappearing into the train car.

Once on the train, he moved to the back of the car and settled into an empty seat. People were talking all around him, or waving out the window. He looked out and waved at his brothers. His family stood on the platform waving while the train filled up. After what seemed like an eternity trapped in limbo, his stomach rolling with nerves and excitement, Auggie felt the train pull forward an inch. They were moving. He was on his way.

The Greives stood on the platform in the early sun, watching as the train slowly began to move forward. They saw Auggie in the window, still waving. "I'll write cha every day!" he shouted. "I love you!" but the whistle of the engine drowned out his words. The train picked up speed and Auggie began to disappear from view. Soon the train was on its way down the line, the platform much emptier than it was before. Mrs. Greive was crying freely now, watching as the train turned into a small dot on the horizon before disappearing entirely.

Auggie settled into his seat and watched the fields roll by. He was excited to get to Ohio and get started, and he was nervous about what to expect. He reached into the pocket of his trousers and felt the familiar folded square of newsprint.

Chapter Four

ARRIVAL IN CINCINNATI

The train grew more crowded as the bright midday faded into evening. The locomotive would slow as it neared the next town, with its platform full of eager young men and heartbroken family members. It was a day for "goodbye" across the state, it seemed, and all the mothers' eyes were wet.

Auggie settled into the cushioned seat after watching people board at the next stop and closed his eyes. His railway car remained, at most, half full, and he was thankful for the quiet on some level. His stomach had stopped churning with the nerves of saying goodbye, and he watched the horizon through the glass and thought about how brave this train was.

The railroad meandered across the state; the cars rocked and lurched as the train progressed. After a while he dozed off in his seat, and woke to see that the final light of the sun was lingering at the edge of the horizon. The train car was softly lit with lamps that made it seem softer and more friendly. He felt a familiar feeling in his stomach—hunger, and realized this was when he would be sitting home to his mother's cooking if he was back at the farm.

Then the rail line started to descend along a small creek. Auggie stared to take notice of the towns as they passed, "Milan," "Cold Springs," "Dillsbourgh," "Cochran." They were now at the bottom of the long grade and came to a stop in Aurora. There it was, the Beautiful Ohio River he had only heard about from the drummers that stop by the general store back home!

After "Lawrenceburgh," they crossed another river and entered Ohio. There were moments when it seemed like the train wanted to race the river. Outside, the river widened and narrowed in view. Shrubs and small trees lined the shores, and occasionally a duck or other waterfowl could be spotted. Auggie wondered if Ohio was really much different than Indiana, and reckoned it wasn't.

Suddenly, as if conjured by magic, an Ironclad Riverboat! The sight caused Auggie to jump from his seat and give out a loud whistle, his first real contact with the war!

He rifled through the sack that he brought on board and found the hard biscuits she had packed him. They were wrapped in a cheesecloth and Auggie shook the loose crumbs from it, watching them tumble to the seat below. He brushed them further, sending them to the floor, before taking a bite of the biscuit.

He felt the familiar pull of the engines slowing. With a mouth full of biscuit, he looked out the window to see if he could see the next platform. It looked like the ones that came before it, with the bright sun shining off the slate roof of the station.

"North Bend!" called out the train's conductor. This was the farthest Auggie had been from home in his entire life.

This time, his car filled with the sounds of boys laughing and talking their way into manhood. A tall blonde boy with a younger version of himself right behind came up to the seat where Auggie sat before looking around.

"This taken?" the older one asked with a voice full of bravado. It was apparent to everyone that the seat was indeed, not taken.

"Not at all," Auggie nodded, shifting as though to give appearance to making room.

The two blonde boys took seats—one next to Auggie and the other directly across. They didn't say anything for a minute, simply staring at each other across the train car, taking each other in. The younger boy, who was across from Auggie, leaned over and pressed his face against the glass.

"Ma's still crying, Cy," he said, looking back at the bigger kid. They both had dusty blonde hair and sharp blue eyes.

"She'll be crying all night and probably tomorrow, too," Cy said, before turning to Auggie.

"Name's Cyrus. This here is Benjamin," he said, nodding at his brother.

"Auggie," Auggie said. He put his hand out and the boys shook.

"Goin to Camp Dennison too, I take it?" Cyrus asked.

"Yes, I am. Finally convinced my parents to let me enlist. My ma was cryin' like yours."

"Didn't have to convince Papa much, but Ma still isn't happy," Benjamin added. "Wasn't sure if they were gonna let Ben come with me at all," Cy said, nodding his head slowly like he was replaying the conversations in his mind.

"I have a brother back on the farm," Auggie said, "he's gotta pull more weight now. My parents are worried about not having me around for the harvest."

"My mother was joking that our sisters would have to get out there and plow the fields while we're gone. The little one started to cry when she said that," Benjamin smiled as he looked out the window.

The train had pulled away from the platform and was speeding up as it moved away from the station and along the river.

"Addyson!" the conductor bellowed.

"How long until we hit Cincinnati?" Auggie asked.

"Not long, now. It will go by fast. Then onward to Camp Dennison." "We have to transfer," Ben added.

"I know that. I was the one that told you that," his older brother playfully scolded.

"I wonder how many people will be at Dennison when we get there," Auggie asked.

"Half of Indiana, and all of Ohio!" Cy laughed and jostled Auggie in the shoulder.

"I saw that train platform. It seems like most of Ohio is staying home to cry!" Auggie wasted no time in responding.

The boys broke into laughter at the exchange and soon they were talking rapidly about their lives on the farm. They all had dreams of being the bravest man on the line, going into battle to protect their country and the freedom that their parents had moved so far away from home to achieve.

"Delhi!"

THERE WAS NO MISSING CINCINNATI ON the horizon—the buildings were taller and clustered together. As the train pulled closer to the outskirts, houses popped up along the tracks. The boys all leaned over to look out the window and try to get the best look first. The city was bigger than any town that Auggie had ever seen, or even imagined. He could tell just by looking at Cyrus and Ben that it was the same for them.

"It's so big," Ben said.

"Way bigger than anything there is in Indiana," Cy said with an eye roll in Auggie's direction.

"Ha! You guys haven't seen a city any more than I have," Auggie replied. They settled back in their seats once more as the train pulled closer to Cincinnati.

"Cinnn-cinnn-naaa-taaah! End of the line!" sang out the conductor.

It finally stopped beside the train depot and the boys stood up and stretched. There was now a nervous excitement that filled the entire car and everyone was jostling to get their bags or look out the window.

"We're gonna have to go across town to the other station for the train to Dennison," Cy said.

"I know. We all know that. Everyone on this train knows that," Ben said. He slung his sack over his shoulder and followed after Cyrus as he headed down the aisle and toward the open door.

The depot was hot and noisy, with people moving around at a great pace. There were fewer tears than had been at any of the stations, but there was a lot of noise. It seemed that there were more porters than passengers at times, and conductors' voices broke over the crowd calling out arrivals and departures.

The boys gathered their sacks and followed the sea of young men through the heavy doors of the depot station and out into the street. If the depot had been noisy and crowded, Cincinnati was ever more so. The street was narrow, and the buildings that lined it were tall and sandwiched together. It looked as though they had run out of space while building, even though Ohio's hills stretched for miles on either side. The noise, smoke and stench of the city made Auggie wish he was back home, inhaling the sweet clean aroma of country living.

Auggie couldn't help but look around to take it all in. There were men crowded along the street, walking to and from the buildings and the depot. They all looked so serious to Auggie. The women looked on at the sea of young men that were traversing the narrow street, with looks of sympathy and admiration. Auggie stood taller and tried to look stronger.

"They love soldiers," Benjamin said, noticing what Auggie did.

"You're not a soldier, yet," Cy teased.

"They like us anyway," Auggie added.

The sky shone a heavy blue through the spaces between the buildings and smoke. The day was nearing its end at this point, and the boys around them all looked tired. The walk across town to the Pearl Street Depot was long and tiresome, and it proved to be more crowded than the first. This one was entirely larger and packed with young men looking to start their grand tenure with the troops. Many had arrived by packet boats up and down the Ohio

River. There was a great deal of shouting and hollering as people organized their belongings and boarded the train that would take them all the final leg of the trip to Camp Dennison. Auggie felt the nerves return to his stomach.

The boys climbed aboard the train and found their seats, slinging their sacks down around them. The rest of the car filled quickly. This part of the trip was already louder than the last. Everyone was talking with voices full of bravado. Loud jokes were flung from seat to seat, and over the heads of anyone who was leaning against the window to get a final look at the city they were rolling slowly out of.

Auggie took a deep breath and sat back. Cy and Benjamin were quiet too, and they looked as tired as he felt. He thought of his mother on the platform that morning, and of their rapid approach to Camp Dennison. He wondered if he had another biscuit in his sack as he tried to stay excited, and awake. In the car ahead, the boys had broken out in song singing "Shouting the Battle Cry of Freedom."

Chapter Five

PREPARING FOR THE STORM

With the Union's arrival in Chattanooga, the air around the Braunhoff General Store and the other small buildings that lined the road had grown heavy with war. It seemed that the only thing on anyone's mind those days was whether and how the fighting might progress. Will had heard his parents talking in hushed tones by the fire one night after he had been sent to bed, and he thought about how the Yankees in Chattanooga were real soldiers, and not squirrels digging for acorns. The next morning after breakfast, Will went outside and plopped down.

"I'm goin' to the store," Will's father's voice broke through his thought.

He looked up from where he was sitting on the front porch. He watched his mother kiss his father lightly on the cheek at the threshold and watched as he took a big step off the porch and into the dirt. Will's father normally would have scolded him for just sitting around when there was work to be done, but lately he was too concerned with the business of the war to get on the boy about how he spent his time. Will's mother seemed happy that he had stuck closer to home lately, glad that he and Sam weren't up on the mountain or getting into trouble. It seemed to be coming without anybody helping it.

The elder Braunhoff walked on down the road with his hands thrust in his pockets, his chin down in deep thought, causing his neatly trimmed beard to rest on his chest. The air was already getting thick and heavy. The morning sun was feeling like the bellows he was passing at Obadiah Washington's blacksmith shop. He knew there would be much conversation today about the troop movements, and he wondered how much of it would be conjecture, and what they should do. The women were getting more anxious, and they were quick to talk amongst themselves after church and on sunny afternoons. Braunhoff wished that they wouldn't, and would just leave the war to the men, even if they didn't want any part of it either.

The General Store stood next to a small barbershop that serviced the locals and those who traveled from the more rural farms for a trim. It served as the place that the men gathered, after stopping off at the store to stock up on supplies, to exchange news and discuss important matters. When Braunhoff reached the barbershop and looked in the thin pane of a window, he saw that everyone was already there. He pulled the wooden door open with a jerk and stepped inside, allowing the other men to move out of his way. They nodded at him and he nodded back.

"Listen, I still don't think Georgia is going to see the arrival of the Union scoundrels. We have nothing to do with this," a voice rang out from the back of the room.

"I think that's short sighted," Tillet said. He was leaning against the wall by the barber's counter, his elbow resting next to a glass jar of combs.

"We're smack in the middle of it," Braunhoff said, adding his voice to the mix. He went to stand next to his friend. The air was heavy in the room and it was obvious that the disagreements ran deep.

"What happens when the fighting is in our yards?" George, a farmer who lived south of the store asked.

"Well, we'll fight, of course! And kill them dead," someone called.

"And they'll kill a few too, I suspect," Braunhoff said. Tillet nodded.

"The women are nervous. They are talking, too, and gossip spreads so fast. They are all nerves now that the Union hit Chattanooga, and I can't blame them," Tillet said. His wife had been over at the Braunhoff house with her sister every afternoon since the news first arrived that the troops were setting up in the grassy fields outside of Chattanooga.

"Brown will keep us out of it. He doesn't think the Confederacy is strong enough to see this through the end and is just involving everyone in their own mess. Ever since Jeff Davis started that overall draft, he's been centralizing all the power in Richmond. What did we declare our independence for in the first place anyway? Davis is as much as a dictator as that damned Lincoln!" George lamented.

"The Hell with Jeff Davis and God Bless Governor Joe Brown!" came an excited shout from the back of the room. Everybody gave a "whoop" of approval.

"I don't think Brown is an ally in this," Braunhoff started. He knew that everyone in Georgia looked to their governor and had considered him to be staunchly against getting involved in the conflict or having his resources decimated for someone else's agenda. Braunhoff thought there was more to his position, though.

"What do you mean by that?" one of the men asked, taking a step closer. "What I mean is that he's got an agenda like anyone," Braunhoff started. A few men shook their heads at him.

"Yeah, the agenda is to keep this war away from us," George said.

"I think he's more a preservationist than that," Braunhoff started, "he doesn't want his state involved in the war because he wants everyone here when the war comes anyway."

"And protecting our homes is a bad thing?"

"Not at all. In fact, we need to do that. That's why we're here, right? What I'm saying is that the war is coming, and if Governor Brown, or any one man could stop the armies, it would be over."

The group around him began to talk in hushed tones amongst themselves. Braunhoff's words hadn't landed well with some of them, and he could see them sizing him up and wondering where he stood.

Tillet stood and watched, next to him. He knew Braunhoff was right, and also knew that either way, protecting their farms, their families, and their resources was going to be key.

"I think you're wrong about Brown," a new dissenter said, with more conviction than George.

"I may be. It doesn't matter, too much, since the war is coming. Any talk here about Brown is keeping us from preparing, and it is divisive. If the country wants war, fine, but we don't need our own civil war here on our main street," Braunhoff raised his voice with the seriousness of someone who needed to be heard.

"Our best bet is to shore up our lands, and make a plan for if the troops do make it this far. No one thought the Union was going to make it to Chattanooga and they have. They might as well be at the door, and soon they will be. Us in the middle? We'll be eaten alive by both sides," Tillet said, shaking his head.

"Right, so what do we do here? We should be hiding our animals, or planning for it. You heard the news last week about the Union buggers going and taking over. Even Davis and his men think the land and all of our hard earned keep belong to them. We'll have nothing left but dead bodies and empty bellies," Braunhoff agreed.

"You're getting wrapped up in the gossip like the ladies," this time it was Joseph, a lanky man who worked at the Lacy Hotel.

"Ha! It's talk like that that has left towns crushed by the damn Yankees. Listen, if the Union gets this close, how can you expect the Confederacy to just hang back? We're going to have them here in this barbershop soon enough, raiding my store next door for their soap and socks!" he stepped forward, now realizing that reason wasn't going to prevail, necessarily.

"Maybe you just care about that, then, the loss of your socks and soap," Joseph nearly spat the words out.

"Everyone should be. Do you want them here, on our streets, digging in? Should our women have to listen to the sound of canon thunder?"

"It's not going to come this far!"

"It already has. We are right in the middle of it. Brown can't stop that," Braunhoff snapped. "They're right at our door in Chattanooga! I know how Sherman thinks; I'm from Ohio too! He's not going to stop until he's crushed us all under the boot!"

"Damned Yankee!" bellowed George as he jumped to his feet, knocking his chair to the floor.

"I'm no Damned Yankee! I'm just as much a Georgian as you are and love my homeland as much as anyone here!" Braunhoff spat, gritting his teeth, and stepping forward with clenched fists.

"Listen, listen," Tillet stepped in between the men, accidentally knocking over the jar of combs as he moved. They clattered to the slatted floor. "We CANNOT turn on each other. Braunhoff cares about the store. You should care about the hotel, and your home, and your family. Plan for the worst. The cannons are coming."

Will had followed his father into town and hesitantly pressed his face against the window to watch the scene. He could tell the men were angry, and their voices rose out of the building. He stepped back, so as not to be seen, and wandered down the road to sit beneath a tree and think about what was happening around him.

Cannons sounded exciting, as did real soldiers, but he could see the fear on his mother's and aunt's faces. He knew everyone thought the mountain would keep them safe, isolate them from the fighting around them. Even Mrs. Lacy, who was always in a good mood, had been somber the last time he brought squirrels over to her. He hoped his father could reason with everyone and bring them around. Though, he did want to see real soldiers. He watched a squirrel across the road and pretended to take aim.

THE SUN WAS BRIGHT ON THE parade ground, and the clouds floated by as though there wasn't a war going on. It was the perfect day for celebrating, and the edges of the field were full of townspeople coming out for the festivities.

"Forward March!" Wilkerson's voice boomed at the troops that were assembled in front of him. Business men, bankers, and the lawyers he worked with had traded their accounts and paperwork to be a part of his militia, and their bravado was obvious as they marched in perfect formation, their weeks' worth of drilling paying off.

The ladies clapped their white gloved hands from where they sat on the grass, as the children ran around. A group of boys occupied the far corner of the field, practicing their own drills, smaller voices calling out for control and direction. At that moment, the war was just a reason to get together as a town and celebrate. Fighting would never reach them, and their men would go off and come back with tales of victory and courage. A bandstand had been erected at the front of the field and draped with red, white, and blue bunting. After the presentation of drills, there would be speeches and recognition. Nell and her mother sat on a duvet, right by the bandstand, with a picnic basket between them.

"They are so handsome, aren't they?" Nell said to her mother, her voice soft with dreams of her life with Robert.

"They are, indeed. Robert looks so valiant, doesn't he?" her mother asked, looking at her with a smile.

"He does. He's going to be such a hero," Nell said, clapping her hands in front of her.

The drills began to wind down. The soldiers marched once more around the field in formation, their boots lifting and landing with exact precision on the dusty field. Their uniforms were starched and the buttons kept catching the sun and sending rays of light spraying across the grass.

"At ease!" the command came forth from Nell's father and the soldiers relaxed, moving into a swarm of fathers and brothers and fiancés as they crossed the field to their families.

Robert walked over to Nell, who rose and embraced him.

"You are so brave!" she exclaimed.

He smiled and tried to look like he was as brave as she said.

"It's easy to be brave, when I know you'll be waiting for me to return," he said. Nell smiled again and felt her heart soar. She looked around and thought about how she had the most handsome soldier of them all. And after the war, he would return to her and they would get married in the church and have a reception in the big parlor at her home. Then he would settle into a career as a lawyer and she would be a doting wife and mother like her own. She couldn't wait until she was entertaining in her own home, looking forward to his daily return from work.

The bandstand was getting busy now, as people assembled closer to it for the speeches to start. Someone moved over a wooden podium borrowed from the school house and set some papers on the front of it. The mayor was the first to speak, an aged businessman who was too old to fight himself. He was young enough to praise the militia though, and rambled in the warm sunlight about the town's bravery and willingness to go help the great country out of the mess of war.

"He has a lot to say," Nell said under her breath.

"You're just anxious," her mother whispered.

Nell was anxious. She was going to present Robert with a sash for his sword, in front of the whole crowd. She was excited, but worried she might faint at all the attention.

Soon, it was time, and she got up from where she sat. She straightened her skirts and walked toward the crate that served as a step up onto the wooden stage. Her father stood next to the podium, between the mayor and Robert. He beamed at his daughter as she unfolded the sash in her hands, its golden hue glimmering.

"Nell Wilkerson's showing her own bravery, letting her father and fiancé go off to war," the mayor said, "and she'd like to make sure that they do that properly."

The crowd clapped as he beckoned her closer.

She looked out at the crowd and smiled, before turning to Robert. He was smiling at her and she felt her heart race again. She held out the sash and curtseyed slightly, as he took out his sword and showed it off in the sunlight. The crowd clapped louder.

"You are so brave," she said, softly.

"You are, my love," he said, taking the sash. He embraced Nell gently before she turned and left the platform to rejoin her mother, a radiant blush emanating from her face.

"You ladies needn't worry," her father said, addressing the group, "you know how good these men are—the best. And now they're the best troops, and they are going to help win this war!" his voice boomed and the crowd cheered.

Sharp whistles echoed across the field and the sun continued to shine.

Chapter Six

THE WATCHED POT BOILS

*A*uggie had a bit of a headache. He was tired. Cy and Benjamin sat across from him, wearing similar faces. They had not slept well the past few days. The nights had been loud as troops talked and planned and prepared for what was ahead. There was a constant harmony of soft, nervous voices bouncing against the bravado and swagger of the others. The mornings were early and the days were long. Auggie closed his eyes for a moment.

There had been a lot of talk in the last day or two about what would meet them when they arrive in Georgia. Troops were coming from all over—including many from the east. Auggie had heard that the troops from up north were colder—battle-worn and aggressive with those who were coming in from points west. He shook it off when he heard it, now used to the rumors that flew amongst the men when there was time for idle chit chat. It was easier, he expected, to talk about the other regiments than to discuss what might happen when they finally came face to face with the Confederates.

"You know we're the best regiment there is," Cy said, with sleepy conviction.

"Yep," his brother replied.

"I wonder how many of us there will be," Auggie said out loud. He pictured rows and rows of troops like them, all getting ready to charge forward. He had told his mother in his letters that he wasn't nervous—but his stomach would suggest otherwise.

"Enough to end this war," Cy answered.

"Them Rebs don't know what's coming for them. We're gonna tear them up and send them running," Benjamin said.

Robert leaned against the seat of the train and looked out the window. He thought about Nell and how pretty she had been when they said goodbye. He knew that she was worried sick about him, and probably letting it get to her. He had sat up the night before writing her a letter to try and calm her nerves and let her know that he was going to be alright. He cared about her deeply, and hoped that it would at least dull the pain of being without him.

The farm land rolled past the window. They were heading to meet up with Sherman and march south. Everyone thought it was time to end the war, and they were hoping that this would be a part of that. Atlanta was key to driving the Confederates back and opening the south. Everyone was confident it would happen. Sherman had been strong so far, and he would lead them to victory again.

His mind drifted again, back to his home in Illinois. Once Atlanta fell, the war should end quickly, and he would be able to get back to his old life. There would be much celebrating when the men returned; the parties would go on for days, filling the evenings with stories of bravery and rekindling of friendships. Nell's father would be a hero, and would certainly be on his way to more prestige and maybe a political office. He would follow in his footsteps, enjoying the success that came with fighting in a war to keep the country together.

As the train got closer and closer to its destination, everyone seemed to sit up straighter. There were low murmurs as they talked amongst themselves, looking out the window to try and catch the first glimpses of other troops. Finally, the train began to slow down, and the station came into view. Robert looked out the window and saw troops moving about in small hoards—having just arrived themselves.

It seemed like the train was taking forever to finally stop, but eventually it did, sliding into the station with its final momentum and then halting with a slight jar, causing the men to jerk forward. Everyone stood up and began to gather their bags, jostling one another into the aisle and toward the end of the car. Nell's father was at the head of the line to get out, his face set in stone as he looked back and nodded at the men who had followed him all the way here from the parade field back home.

Robert took a deep breath and adjusted his shirt. He waited while the other men filed out around him and there was a margin of space to step into the aisle without shoving. The men were laughing and talking loudly as they left the train, gaining swagger with every step. They filed into the bright sunlight of the afternoon and looked around.

"Illinois has arrived," someone said behind him.

"Time to drive the devils back," another voice called out.

Robert stayed quiet, but nodded his head with each call from the crowd. He was proud to be here with these men, and he knew that they were the absolute best that the country had to offer. There was no reason to be nervous because they were going to go in full force and show them what it meant to be a soldier.

THE CAMP WAS HUGE, WITH TENTS and soldiers occupying most of the space. Auggie looked around at everyone and realized how many of them were actually there. Even though the entire way to Chattanooga they had talked about the forceful assault they were about to be a part of, he had not pictured what that many people actually looked like. From all around, whoops and hollers rang out through the air as men talked victory, and told stories from their homes. It seemed almost jovial, and Auggie found himself smiling a bit with the energy that seemed to be in the air.

"There's no way to lose with this many of us," Benji said.

"There sure seem to be more people than I could ever count," Auggie said, "there has to be more of us than there are of them."

"Atlanta isn't going to go down without a fight. It'll take all of us to get this done right," Cy said. He looked around excitedly at the different regiments.

"Where you all from?" a soldier asked them, looking up from his rations. "Ohio," Auggie answered. "Actually Indiana myself." "What about you?" Cy asked.

"Illinois. We arrived by train a while ago. Didn't think there's be so many of us." "Neither did we. But it makes us feel good right? Look at how many people are here for the cause," Cy said.

"Well, I think some of them might be here for their own pride," the soldier said, "one of the regiments from the east was howling viciously earlier about their accomplishments on the field."

"Good for them. They haven't seen what we've got yet!" Benji slapped his palm on his thigh for emphasis as he said it. Auggie had to hold back a laugh at his enthusiasm. He had been relatively quiet the whole way from Cincinnati, but now was showing his bravado.

"Surely they will find themselves tempered in battle," the soldier said, nodding his head. "I'm John, by the way," he added.

"I'm Auggie. This here is Benjamin, and his brother Cy," he nodded at the other two before turning back to John. Around them, the boasting grew louder, with more voices joining every moment.

Auggie and the others followed John's lead and settled down with the rest of the regiment to have something to eat and to get ready for the march that was going to come soon. Cy stood watching troops walk by, sizing them up and studying how they moved about the crowd. He would occasionally comment on a soldier to the others, noting how young he looked, or how ill prepared he was to go into bloody battle. Auggie would nod when it seemed appropriate, but he knew his friend was nervous and trying to focus on something that wasn't so serious.

More and more troops joined them and the field grew more crowded and louder. Once everyone was there, it would be time to fall in and begin the assault.

People were panicking now. Big Shanty and Marietta were buzzing with folks preparing for the troops that were on their way to the front. Up until now, it had been easy to think that the war might not get to them. It was clear now that was not the case, and soon the battle would be raging around them. The general store seemed to always be full now, with people buying supplies and gathering to try and make sense of what was going on around them.

The train station was busier than it had ever been, with trains pulling in night and day to unload Confederate soldiers and the supplies they would need to defend the mountain that stood between them and the impending Union forces. Will and Sam would occasionally sneak off to watch from a distance as the men got off the train, calling back and forth amongst themselves as they unloaded and carried weapons and supplies.

Will's mother had told him to stop going out to the station to watch the soldiers, worried he would get himself in a bad situation. Will had nodded and agreed to keep away, knowing that he wouldn't obey that particular order. The battle hadn't started yet, so there couldn't be any danger more than getting caught by his mother.

"When do you think it will happen?" Sam asked. They were on their way back from the station, having just watched another round of men stream out of the cars. These men looked like they had seen some battle already—Will could see their weariness even from a distance.

"When do I think what will happen?" Will asked.

"The battle. When is it going to start, ya think?"

"Hopefully not for a while yet. It seems like they still have work to do," Will nodded his head back in the direction they had come from.

"Yeah. But it has to be soon. I mean, look at everyone at the store these days. It's like they've lost their minds. I'm half surprised Ma hasn't kept me in the house all day."

"They're all worried. The soldiers make them nervous. I don't think the battle will make it this far. Our boys will keep them at bay, but the adults have to worry about what happens if they come through."

"I think the soldiers are exciting," Sam said.

"Me too."

They continued their walk along the road toward the general store. As it came into view, they could see that their mothers were sitting on the porch outside, talking to some of the other local women. As they got closer they could hear the worry in their voices as they all talked over one and other. Mrs. Tillet, in particular, looked concerned. She shook her head back and forth as she spoke.

"I know the men have started to hide the horses and mules, which is good. But what about the children? Some of us have talked about them. Maybe we should be hiding them as well," she said. A few women nodded.

Will and Sam came up the step and onto the porch, nodding at their mothers. They quickly slipped into the store, letting the door close behind them. Inside the store, Mr. Braunhoff stood behind the counter with his arms crossed. He was deep in thought and didn't look up at first when the boys came in.

"Hello, boys," he said once he realized they were standing there.

"Hello," Will said to his father.

"What have you two been doing? Hopefully not bothering your mothers. They seem agitated enough without help," he said.

"We were down by the pond, throwing rocks," Will said.

"That sounds good. Your mother wants you close to home. Make sure you remember that," his father said.

The door opened and two men came in, talking about the Confederate soldier they had run into earlier in the day. They stopped their conversation and began to gather supplies from the shelves. Mr. Braunhoff scowled as one of them knocked over a box of matches as he reached for something behind it. This was becoming a regular occurrence in the store—customers coming in with panic on their faces and no regard for keeping the shelves organized. He had never spent so much time reorganizing supplies, and picking up those that had been bumped or discarded on the wrong shelf.

"Let's hope there aren't many more soldiers coming down this way. It will scare all the women. They're already panicked. If you go out there and listen to them, they are sure the world is about to end," the taller man said, shaking his head at his friend and Mr. Braunhoff.

"Are they still talking about hiding the children?" Will's father asked.

"Yeah. They're terrified that the fighting will run into town. I told them they didn't need to worry about that," the man said.

"The soldiers won't make it this far. Hiding the pigs and horses is one thing, they might get poached by the forces. Or stolen in the night. But, the children are safe as long as they stay close to town," Mr. Braunhoff said, turning toward his son as he said it.

"Their mothers will all be keeping them indoors soon, I suspect," the shorter man said with a laugh as he stacked his wares on the counter. Mr. Braunhoff began to package them up and total his price.

Will and Sam slipped behind the counter and through the door into the back room. Sam's father sat at a desk, looking over a ledger. He looked up when they came in.

"I thought I heard you," he said.

"We got tired of throwing rocks into the pond. Apparently the two men out there met a Confederate soldier today," Sam told his father.

"I've seen one myself. They are coming through every so often, it seems." "Did you talk to him?" Sam asked.

"No. I just saw him as he was walking down the road back to the mountain. It may have been the same one that those folks saw," he replied.

"When do you think the battle is going to start?" "I still hope it doesn't," he said.

Outside, the women were still talking about hiding their children so that nothing could happen to them. Mr. Braunhoff stepped outside to listen to the conversation for a moment, but could only stand there a brief time, as people kept coming into the store looking to buy supplies. Inside, he listened to everyone talk in panicked voices about what might happen in the coming days. Mr. Tillet came out of the back office and helped pack up everyone's purchases. Before leaving for the night, both men went out and straightened the shelves, which looked like they had been ransacked by criminals.

Mr. Braunhoff returned home and sat down at the table with his wife. She looked worried.

"What do you think about this notion of hiding the kids? Will?" she asked her husband.

"I don't think it's necessary. Hide the horses, yes. The children are fine. Just keep them close. Even at home, if that makes you more comfortable," he said, sighing a bit. He knew his wife was scared, but he was exhausted by everyone's panic around him.

"Alright. If you really think he's okay," she said, nodding.

"I do. Everything is going to be fine. I told Will to listen to you and keep close to home. I don't want him wandering off and getting into trouble."

"Good. I reminded him at breakfast to stay away from the train and the mountain. No hunting for squirrels."

Mr. Braunhoff woke up early the next morning and made his way to the store to get some work done before customers started arriving. Tillet arrived soon after, and the men worked in quiet for a while. It was soon time to open up, and once they did there were men in the store immediately.

"Did you hear?" Mr. Clark asked, leaning on the counter and looking at Braunhoff.

"About what?" he asked.

"They're heading for Atlanta and it looks like they might be able to take it.

They really are going to make it to the mountain," he said.

"No, they won't. That's just talk. Atlanta will hold," another man said. "Doubtful. And what's more, I hear they're destroying the railway as they come through," Mr. Clark said.

"I've heard that too," a voice added.

"The key to winning any war is who can get the supplies to the front," Mr. Braunhoff said, "burning the train line will make it hard for the confederates to use it if they need it." The men nodded.

"Still, I think Atlanta will hold."

"Let's hope you're right," Braunhoff said, worrying for a moment himself that the war might get too close to home. "But don't forget, they still have to get past us to be able to get to Atlanta!"

Everyone just looked at one another with a blank stare as reality slapped them in the face full force.

Too close to home, too close to home.

Chapter Seven

FROM THE FRONT

Dearest Mama and Papa,

I hope this letter finds you well. I am as healthy as can be, and remain in good spirits. There are a number of men here who have family that are Old World Deutsche. It is very much like being at home, sometimes. It's almost easy to forget the formidable task ahead of us, but we stay focused on that. The first few days were so strange, and so different from life on the farm. I guess I had expected that, but it was still a shock. Some handled it far worse than others, though they tried to hide their emotions behind stone faces.

I do miss you, Mama. I didn't realize how much I missed the farm until I wasn't out in the fields each day. We've seen so many different things since leaving the city, farms, and towns. The country is so big, and it's such a shame that it's being torn apart by those scoundrel Rebels now.

All the more important that I go forth and do this. I don't want you or Papa worrying about me. I am brave and ready to do my best to protect the beautiful land that we call home. Tell my brother I miss him too, and I send all my love.

Your Loving Son,
August H. Greive
52nd Ohio

To: August Greive,

Auggie! We are comforted and glad to hear that you are managing well out there. I try and stay away from the dark feelings of worry, but sometimes it is hard. The house is empty without your footsteps. Papa misses you too, though he tries to be more serious about it. There is a chill in the air and I wonder if you are warm and fed enough, or just trying to calm my mind about you. It can't be a simple feat to feed the lot of you. You're still growing boys, with growing appetites.

Your father loves you and wishes you safety. He is proud of you and your conviction to the cause you believe in. Never doubt that, Auggie, even if he was cross when you decided to become a brave soldier boy. There is pride in fighting for what you believe in, even if it keeps your mother awake in the late hours of the night. Your brother has picked up your lot of chores on the farm, and he is working hard to show that he can do it all. I dare say you will owe him something when you return!

Eat. Rest as much as you can, and remain calm and strong. I look forward to your next letter, and hope that you will soon be reunited with your home and your family.

Always,
Mama

My Dearest Mama and Papa,

There is great camaraderie amongst us enlisted men and it makes up for the loneliness we might feel when thinking about home. Cyrus and Benjamin from the train remain my closest confidants in the field. There is also George, who is from Yellow Springs, Ohio. He's a giant— nearly two of me, and so soft spoken one must lean in terribly close to hear what he is saying. I call him "Pferd," but I don't say it too often because it would hurt him if he understood it was "horse" in German. The whole regiment has gotten closer as we've been getting nearer to the front.

News comes in from the front and it sombers us at times. The rebels are tearing up the country and while we are a brave bunch, the union isn't winning every battle. I am sure you know this. I hope Pa is keeping you from worrying too much. The biggest rumor by the fires at night is that the war will be over soon. The rebels are spirited, but we are going to take it, and have the righteous cause behind us!

In the evenings, after camp has been set and supper done, we sit around and tell stories from home. Cy and Benjamin's story of their mother reminds me so much of you, Mama. One day when all of this is behind us good, I would like to keep in contact with them—they are good men.

The air gets hotter every day, Mama. If it didn't feel like we were steppin' into the pits of hell, the stories from the front make it clear. I don't want to worry you, but the rebels are digging in as they know we're coming for them. It will be over soon and I will be home again, sitting at the table eating biscuits. My pencil dulls and I want this ready to go out in the morning, so it is g'night for now, Ma.

All my love,
August H. Greive

Dearest Mama,

I am writing this somberly. The weight of the Union defeat at Chickamauga, last September, has all of us heavy hearted and worried. We will be in Georgia, with General Sherman soon ourselves, and would have liked to arrive as the rebels were retreating. Men here are quiet for the losses they know they will hear about, the violence and the senselessness of the rebellion more apparent than ever. I keep faith that I will be delivered from this safely, and I do not want you to worry, ever.

I am sure they fought valiantly. They were worn from the long trek across the state, rumor was they were pushing too hard to make up for time. Going to battle in exhaustion seems like trying to fight in quicksand. I dare say I understand the tired though—the days are long, and even simple movements are often complicated by the sheer number of us. If the farm ever seemed crowded—well, this is the kind of crowded where you can smell men's fear and sadness mixed with the heavy air.

At night we still try to think of home and to keep our spirits up. It is comforting to know the moon we look upon is also being seen by folks back home. With the news of the defeat so heavy on our hearts, that has been especially hard. Ben has become quiet. He used to laugh more than any of us. I can hear him sometimes at night talking to Cy. At least they have each other out here.

I am thankful for your last letter. It cheered my spirits to hear about Papa's crops, and your church picnic. I wish I had been there to eat your delicious food. I miss your fried chicken and fresh dandelions wilted with bacon grease. Was Katherine Gregory there? I've been thinking of her lately. I will be back soon. Remember, this fight is to protect the lives and values we hold so dear to us, and keep the Union as a whole. I think of you daily.

All my love,
August H. Greive

Dear Auggie,

 I cannot tell you how much your mother misses you here on the farm. I do too, of course, but she longs deeply for the day that you are again at her table. Your brother John is doing a fine job of holding up the farm with me. He's gotten stronger and quicker and looks more and more like you, my son. I am proud of you both. I know that the days must be getting frightening for you, and more exciting. I pray nightly that you do not see the worst of battle, if the war still rages. Your mother has sent a letter as well, longer than this, I suspect. You are brave, son. Do not fear what is ahead of you, but think of us at home.

Love,
Papa

To my Mama and Papa,

 We will be falling in with the other regiments tomorrow. Camps can be seen throughout the hills. There is renewed vigor amongst my regiment as we look forward to becoming part of something bigger. There is hope by some that there will be familiar faces tomorrow from back home, or places they've been. I am looking forward to meeting new people and finding out how their soldier life has been so far.
 It's been the first day that the weight of the fighting hasn't hung over our heads. Coming into camp was so refreshing, for a moment we could forget what we were joining up to do. Even Benjamin seemed to be renewed in his faith for the army and the men in it. It is a powerful thing to see us all called to cause and ready to take action. That we all keep marching, after the losses at Chickamauga, knowing it only make

our need more dire. The country needs to be restored so that it can begin to heal the losses its bled out on its hillsides.

We feasted tonight, in what way we could, to celebrate meeting up with the others tomorrow. Sherman is a fine leader from what has been said, and if anyone is going to give enough hell to beat back the rebels, it is him. I am proud to be a part of this group of fine soldiers. There won't be another defeat like Chickamauga. There can't be. The union of our great nation depends on it.

I am sure you are worrying more and more, Mama. But please, I beg you, do not. I am in the company of strong character and we share a conviction to do what is morally right. It is how we will protect our families, and our country. I miss you every day and think about all the things I will have to tell you when I return. These letters don't do it justice, and pencils remain in short supply. Tell my brothers and Papa that I think of them too, and that I do miss the farm work.

This war will be over soon, Mama, and I will be home again. Tomorrow is going to be a bright day, and a rallying one for us and our cause. I am going to sleep now, to rest up for what lay ahead.

Your loving son,
August H. Greive

Chapter Eight

HELL COMES TO GEORGIA
AND SATAN'S IN THE SADDLE

News began to trickle in from North Georgia, and what was being said caused great concern to the men at the general store. The only thing anyone discussed anymore was the war and the what would happen if the fighting came to them. Even as the men leaned against the wooden counters in the shop and wondered what battle would look like, they had all assumed they would be more insulated from the war.

"General Joe Johnston will stop that damned Sherman! Y'all jest wait an' see!" a farmer said, handing over some coins to Braunhoff.

"Yes, but it seems that hasn't been the case," Braunhoff replied.

"No matter, they still won't make it this far. This whole war is going to be over soon, anyhow," the farmer said, waving his hand like they were talking about a bothersome fly and not the arrival of troops.

Braunhoff nodded. He looked around the store. The sense of panic had descended finally, it seemed, on everyone. People came in and looked at the shelves like they had something to buy, when they were really just trying to be close if news came. Even the boys had been keeping nearer to the store or the house, afraid to adventure too far into the woods they knew and loved. Everything was different.

"There shoulda been no way for them to make it. Just none," a man called out as he pulled open the heavy door and stepped inside. Tillet wasn't far behind him.

"It's what they're saying though. I thought it was nonsense too, but the story hasn't changed," Tillet replied. He was somber.

Braunhoff came out from behind the counter and joined the men in the front of the store.

"What's that?" he asked, though he already knew. Everyone knew. "Sherman. Spent days checkin' to see where he could bust through. Nothin' a line of Confederates that shoulda held. But somehow, the Yankees managed." Braunhoff looked at Tillet. They had heard, of course, when the news first began to come into town. It had been easy to dismiss the first few days, but no longer.

Their customer busied himself with looking at supplies on the shelves, which were getting emptier quicker as people began to worry. There was a moment of silence as the men stood there, watching.

"It's gonna be hard to keep everyone calm," Tillet said.

"I know. It's already a storm at home."

"The women were all talkin' the other day and they've worked each other up." "They're just scared," Braunhoff kicked his toe into the ground. "Everyone is, it seems."

It seemed that everyone stopped by the store that day, all looking to hear about Resaca. Instead of the passionate arguments from the earlier weeks, the conversation had a different tone. It was obvious that they were not as protected from the battle as they had thought, and that the war wasn't ending yet.

The boys sat under a tree behind the general store and watched the commotion around them. From a new set of eyes, everything would have seemed fine—people milling about on the street outside of the store, doing business and going about their day. The energy was different. There was suddenly a panic, even if it was still a quiet one at that point.

Will heard it at home too, when his parents talked. His mother was scared— he could see it, even when she tried to mask it. His father was calmer, but even he was beginning to wear the stress on his face. He kicked the dirt up with his shoe and watched it resettle.

"You saw the soldiers?" Sam asked. His voice was quiet and heavy with thought. "Yup. Few of us did. They're preparin'. Just like when we get ready to go out and get the Yankee squirrels."

Will watched his friend as he scanned the horizon, looking for them himself.

"They look just like people," Will said.

"I know. I still wanna see."

The boys settled into silence once again as they watched everyone come and go around them. The sky was getting dark above them, with heavy clouds rolling in from over the trees at the base of the mountain. The air was heavy with the rain that wanted to come, and it made the desperation in the air more apparent.

"We can go watch them, when they start to move in," Will said.

THE NEXT FEW DAYS WERE FILLED with rain, and soldiers. The Confederates began to file into the town in larger numbers, wearing faces of weary soldiers. People weren't sure whether to watch them with admiration or dread at what might be coming down the line. They went right to work at the base of the mountain, getting ready to defend it from the Union.

Will and Sam stepped quietly along the side of the road, up into the cover of the trees. They had left the general store when the rain stopped and no one was looking. Will's heart thumped as they maneuvered through the trees. He knew just the spot where they could settle in and watch the preparation without causing a disturbance or being pulled home by one of their mothers.

Sam followed right behind him, looking back occasionally. They could hear the sound of men calling through the woods as they got closer. Will stepped over a root and headed toward a clearing in the trees. He looked down at the slope of hill below him and the road that wound along in the distance.

Men were digging in the dirt with shovels, their backs bent and their eyes focused on the ground before them. Nobody noticed the boys as they settled in to watch. They pulled the earth from the ground and moved it, digging a deep pit. The rains had stopped earlier in the day, but the ground was still wet from all that had fallen in the days before. Each shovel of mud was heavy, and the ground they were digging filled back in with more. The task was never-ending, and the men grunted with the labor.

Will turned at the sound of a tree falling and saw it disturb the branches in the distance as it came down. Men were sawing down trees and dragging the logs up to fortify the mountain. It was even harder labor than the shoveling, and the boys could tell. Soldiers dragged and carried the felled trees through the brush and forest, clearing a path behind them. They were covered in sweat, and panting so hard it was visible from the spot behind the rock.

"Awful," Sam said, nodding at the sweating figures bent and trudging below them.

"Hard work, this war," Will replied, nodding his head with a sobriety that belong more to an older man.

"They're tearing up the mountain," Sam said.

"They're securing it. The Union's been giving them hell. They want to give it back They will, too."

"Maybe. They said that about Chattanooga and now this," he looked out once more.

"Yeah, but a battle's a battle. It just makes the women crazy and the town busy. It will be over soon and all we'll have to worry about is getting squirrels down to the hotel," Will said.

The sun rose higher over the mountain and made the air heavy as the rain dried off of the trees and ground around them. Will wiped sweat from his own brow. Their cotton shirts were heavy with sweat and moisture and clung to their bodies.

The rain and the mud had brought out the mosquitos and flies, too—the air hummed with tiny wings as they assaulted anybody they could find. The boys slapped them away as best they could. Sam scratched the spots that rose up when he missed. The troops below were not spared either—they worked in a cloud of bugs, trying to swat them away as best they could while digging and chopping. The temperature crept slowly higher and higher until everything felt like it was melting. The spring had been warm so far, and wet, but this was the hottest day they had seen since last summer. It weighed on everyone, making them sluggish as they fought the desire to sit and rest.

There was no breeze either. The mountain was still—animals had taken cover far away from the noise and commotion that now filled their home. The trees were still. Even the clouds had gone away briefly, leaving only the open sky and sunlight. It was miserable. And the battle hadn't even started. This was the hottest and wettest June in anyone's memory.

There was a new sound, an even heavier one that began to be heard by the boys. Will stood up and looked to see what it was, trying to place where he was hearing it. Sam looked too. After a minute, it was apparent: Slowly, men were dragging a cannon up from the road. It sat on low wheels that did not want to cooperate with the mud, and the men pulling it along looked worse than everyone around them. Their uniforms hung heavy to their skin, drenched in sweat and covered in mud. Their faces were serious and unflinching, focused only on putting the next foot down and getting the cannon to its destination.

Will followed their path with his eyes, looking up the rise of stone and dirt that was the mountain. They were still at the bottom, where the road just barely began to rise into a slope. Dragging it through the forest and up the side of a mountain would be near impossible. Will watched as they forced the cannon through the least muddy spots of the field. It got stuck, and got stuck again. Most of the process was the men painstakingly loosening the heavy beast from the mud before rolling it forward a foot to start over.

"They're going to take it up," Will said, articulating the awe he felt.

"That's nuts. They can barely get it through the mud," Sam replied.

"Yeah, but they gotta. So they will."

The boys sat there for a little longer before Sam finally said they should head back. They made their way back how they had come, but with less concern for making noise. The whole afternoon they had sat up under the tree and not a single solider paid them any attention. Finally, they reached the road and stepped out from the forest. The sun was lower now, but still hot, and the boys began to trudge toward town.

They saw a wagon approaching from the edge of town. As they got closer they could make out the soldiers flanking either side, leading it to the mountain the boys had just left. Packed in the back of the wagon were slaves- at least a dozen of them, with their heads looking down. The boys stopped and watched as the wagon trundled past them. No one in the back of the wagon said a word. Will watched sweat bead off their skin and roll away. The soldiers on either side of the wagon were talking amongst themselves and swatting away the flies.

The familiar drops of rain hit Will's head and he looked up to see that clouds were rolling in. It would protect them from the sun, a bit, but the last thing anyone needed was mud. The wagon passed them and the boys kept walking. Within moments another wagon appeared, similarly filled with dark bodies hunched over in the back. One or two looked at the surroundings as they passed. Will could see a third wagon coming not far beyond that one, and looked at Sam.

"So many," he said.

"I know. I've never seen this many," Sam said.

"I guess they need someone to help with all that back there," Will cocked his head. "They're gonna be digging and chopping and dragging."

Each wagon was like the one that went before it. They were quiet, with no one saying a word. Nobody made eye contact with the boys, who had stopped to watch and count the faces. They didn't know what to say, but stood there still, until the last wagon passed them. The rain was falling a little harder now, a light drizzle, but in the distance the sun could still be seen peeking from the clouds. Finally, the last wagon had disappeared around the bend and the boys were broken from their trance.

"There are so many people here now," Will said. The town had come alive as the soldiers moved in. The stoop outside the general store had a small crowd around it at any time. Everyone was talking in the hushed voices of panic as they watched the army prepare for war.

OBADIAH JOHNSON WATCHED AS THE WAGONS of slaves began to pass by. He had known, somewhere, that it was only a matter of time before the soldiers would come. To see the army of slaves they brought with them was a different thing all together. He stood outside of his shop dressed in his leather apron; his arms crossed with his heavy hammer clutched in his right hand and his eyes taking it all in.

They all wore the same look of suffering. There was no doubt that they had been in those wagons for miles and miles, and that they had already done more than their fair share of digging. He sighed. He tried to look at each one for a moment as they passed, but it was hard. One body ran into another. He thought back to his own days in leg irons.

There wasn't a day that he didn't revisit his past, but the wagons made it more vivid for him in that moment. He thought back to the feeling of being enslaved, of having no rights or recourse in the world. It had been his normal, for a long time, and it was easy to get comfortable in his new life. He had fared better than most ever would—the man who owned his freedom was one of the better ones. He had always appreciated Obadiah and his intelligence, let him work more and more closely with him. There had been a kindness about him that was distant, but it made things bearable.

When the opportunity had come to buy his freedom, he had never been so happy. His master had allowed him to earn money on the side with his smithing, and he had saved the earnings away with care. Buying freedom would mean being separate from his family, but it allowed him the opportunity to free them as well.

He had never been forced to prepare a mountain for the onslaught of human destruction. But he had been forced to buy his own family. Since then, he had worked to move them beyond those days. Setting up his own shop gave him purpose. He knew the soldiers coming in had different ideas, too, about slavery and the idea of a freed slave. He looked at the procession with storms in his eyes that matched the one on the horizon.

He thought about the war and the men going to fight it. The people who lived here were rallying with them. The last thing they wanted was the Union pouring over the mountain and down the road into town. He was a part of the town and a part of that conversation, but the slaves made him pause. Supporting the troops meant supporting the wagons of slaves they were carting into the quagmire at the base of the mountain.

As the last wagon passed, Obadiah exhaled a low grunt and turned. Outside his shop, he returned to his work replacing a loose shoe on the horse of Colonel Samuel Adams, 33rd Alabama, Army of the Confederate States of America.

Chapter Nine

ILLINI CORRESPONDENCE

My Ever Loving Elizabeth,

I carry you constantly on my mind as we travel farther and farther from home and closer to the heart of this mess. You and Nell are the light that guides me along, and I think that for all of my courage, it is you that are bravest. I know it must not have been easy for you to see us off, and to be left alone on the parade field with Nell and the weight of our family on your shoulders. I know that the house must be lonely and that even the conversations after church must be around the absence of all of the men.

This was is bigger than any of us and it is impossible to forget that as I see more and more sights pass before my eyes that I never considered possible. There is a darkness that settles in man's heart, and I have seen the glimpses of it as we pass those who have been once to Hell already. The courage to fight for a cause is easy to come by when the purpose is so clear.

I am proud of my men and what I have seen of them so far. While there have been moments of private wavering, they have followed me directly and without hesitation. They are good, loyal men and strong enough that no one will take them down. I can see they are driven by the taste of victory, and the anticipation of returning home to a bigger band than when we left.

This war, while gruesome and unrelenting in its devastation, will mean a better future for us. Not only will we live in a nation that rose and rallied for justice and decency, but Springfield will be stronger when we return. The lessons we've learned out here will make us better men — more able to make decisions and think with a clear head.

I have been in constant correspondence with the Republican heads back home. All the ducks are starting to line up for the next Governor's bid. The boys in Chicago are behind me and it looks as if Alton and Quincy are joining in. All I need is one good heroic showing in a big battle that will capture headlines in Springfield, and I'll have the nomination cinched. Then a victory in November should be certain. You will be happy when I am finally home and we are getting ready to go to the first dinner at the Governor's Mansion. We'll have many visits to make after the victory, and you will find your calendar is full of teas and socials. After all of the struggle you're facing now without me, there will be so much celebration.

Hold Nell for me. Tell her Robert is braver than he will let on, and that we will be home before she knows.

Always,
Your loving husband.

My Sweetest Nell,

I miss the way your laugh rang out like a bell when we would sit on your porch and talk. There is no sound that I would rather here right now, and I think about it nightly before losing myself to the dreams of you. I know you must miss our afternoons the same, and I know you must worry—but don't.

I am driven by my love for you—it is the fire that burns every day that the sun rises, and it will bring me home to you and our life together. Nothing could stop the power between us, my sweet, beautiful darling. When we are reunited, our wedding will be the talk of the entire county. Our love will be what others look to model, and we will grow in it.

The sunset the other night captured me and took my breath away. It was so beautiful and all that my mind would allow was the thought of how much more beautiful it would have been if I was sharing it with you, my love. Consider all the sunsets that we will share when I come home to you a hero. I count the moments until I can hold your precious little hand and feel its warmth in my own. You are more amazing that you will ever understand, my Nell.

Thank you for your last letter, it was the nicest thing I have read since leaving, and I hope that you will write me more. They will have to sustain me until we are reunited.

Soon, soon, soon. We will be together, my dear, and our love will flourish. Until then, hold me in your heart.

Love Forever,
Robert.

To my Husband,

Nell and I are holding strong. Nell is worried, and I can see it in her eyes. She waits for the letters from you and Robert with every breath. I have told her that she is making it worse for herself— she needs the distraction of other girls to keep her mind from wandering to Robert. He has been good at keeping the details out of his letters, and just calming *her nerves. It will be wonderful when they are reunited and I can stop worrying like a mother hen about her.*

I worry about you, too, though less than I do her. I know you are made of the strength and character to come through this shining and ready for the next step. Church on Sunday is quieter with the men gone. Of course, that doesn't stop the women from gathering afterward for cake, but all we talk about is what it is like on our own. You would be proud of my strength—Mrs. Carson broke down last week, sobbing like a banshee. I brought over tea yesterday to check on her. She is not faring well. Nerves were never her strength, but it's more apparent now.

It feels girlish to say, but I cannot wait for you to return so that I can dance with such a fine leader at the first victory party! It will be so different when you are back, and we are out being social. I have told Nell the same— to think about the pretty dresses and fancy evenings we will have. If they excite me, they should motivate her as well.

I fall asleep thinking about you gallantly leading your men, charging the ramparts, your sword stabbing forward as you wave your men to victory with the flag of our glorious Union unfurled beside you. I know the glint in your eyes when you are directing others and I imagine it is quite bright out there on the field. I tell the women often that they must know their men are in the best regiment they could be in. They have a selfless, brilliant leader to keep their husbands safe and return everyone home. Nobody is better suited for the task you face than you are, my love. Keep yourself safe. Know we are thinking about you every moment.

Your loving wife.

My brave Robert!

You cannot imagine my sadness; sitting here on the porch you speak of, knowing you are not here with me right now. Mother has tried to keep me distracted with talk of our wedding, but that means nothing when you are so far away and in the grip of danger. I know you are brave, as is my father. But I worry about you every moment that I am not thinking fondly of our last conversations, our last afternoon together.

Your words fill my heart and nourish me, and I need them like I need air. I read each one over, and then store it. I revisit them when I find my heart sinking so low that I might cry. There has never been a love that burns like mine for you, and that you are so far away is the greatest tragedy of my life. It is unfair that I should have to let you go, but I know your bravery is needed by the country now. I try to stay strong.

The other girls don't understand. They chatter like children, but they don't know the loss of being away from you. Hopefully they never know this sadness and longing. I wouldn't wish it on anyone.

Robert, I love you the way the gentle breeze loves the trees in the early morning. I think about the things we will talk about when you come home—the afternoon walks we will take as I tell you everything you have missed. I am afraid I might forget something, but none of that is as important as not forgetting you. I think about your face each night before I sleep—picturing the green of your eyes and the way you light up when we are together. There will never be a man on this earth that is meant for me the way you are—our love is what artists paint about. It is the love of poems, though I can write none that would do it justice.

I don't want to stop writing, but mother is calling me down. I wait every day for your next letter, and will wait tomorrow even though I know this will not get to you for days. Know that our hearts beat as one, and I look only to the beautiful life we will have when you return for good.

All of my love,
Your sweet Nell.

Chapter Ten

BLUE TIDE A COMIN'

Once the rain had started, it didn't end. It fell gently at times, barely grazing the tree tops before landing on the mountain below. Other times the wind and power kicked up and the rain poured, pounding down the long grasses in the field and leaving everybody's boots muddy. The gray skies matched the mood that had settled over the people who called Kennesaw home.

Everyone felt the fear and anxiety, like the dampness that had crept into their bones. The soldiers had grown more numerous by the day, until the point where it was no longer a story to have seen one wandering down the muddy lane toward the general store or back to where the trains from Atlanta rolled in. They were a part of the backdrop of the day now, and as their number grew, so did the nervous chatter and quiet stares from those who were sure that the town was about to succumb to the battle to end all battles.

The rain brought out the bugs, which seemed to dart between the drops on their way to bite anyone they could find. Will and Sam wore the welts and stings across their legs and necks, and even their mothers were caught swatting and scratching furiously when nobody was thought to be looking. Many of the women had taken to staying inside more, keeping even closer to home than they had been. They moved their conversations to each other's' homes instead of setting up on the broad porch of the general store, as had been their custom.

While concern grew, there was also a new undercurrent of excitement. Some people, having seen the inevitability of the battle's arrival, had embraced it, and were now watching with keen and curious eyes as the arming of the mountain continued around them. The boys had been watching since the very first trains rolled in, so they had become experts at the scene as it unfolded around them. It was still new for most of the others though, and some of them began to approach the mountain with trepidation to get a better look at the building of a battlefield.

The trains rolled in furiously now, laden down with more lumber and supplies and slaves to move it all. The small station at the foot of the mountain had been organized now into a supply base for the Confederates, with everything stacked and ready for mobilization to the front. There was a constant chorus of voices that rose from the station and filled the air as men fell in and got organized.

Will and Sam took the long way through the woods to their lookout spot, which was now trampled from their near daily visits to see what was going on and report back to the other boys that weren't brave enough to follow. On their way up to the rock that afternoon, they passed by another two men who had wandered in from town to watch themselves. They wore a look of a surprise at the amount of grunting, growling, shouting and swearing that came from the men who were arming the hill.

The rain had been pouring for an eternity, and the side of the mountain that the troops were calling home showed it. Where the ground had been dug up when they first started clearing the path for the cannon, there was now a soggy, muddy river that ran back down past the troops as they slogged up the hill against its current, with rain soaking their wool uniforms.

"The rain must be miserable!" Sam said, looking over the scene below before turning to face Will.

"Yep. The rain is awful for us, isn't it? And we've spent most of the last week trapped in the house with our mothers." Will scratched a welt on his neck left by a hungry mosquito. It was impossible, at this point, to tell where the rain ended and the sweat began.

"I thought I might go mad if I was inside one more afternoon."

"Both of us would have. And then what good would we be come squirrel hunting season," Will laughed.

The men below that had come up to watch heard the laughter and looked up from their own conversation to see the boys sitting on the rock above them. For a moment, Will was sure he was going to get told to go on home now, back to his parents'. The man below surprised him, and simply shook his head knowingly before turning back to watching the soldiers trudge up the mountain.

The Union had arrived just up "The State Road" and was heading their way! That was the word when the boys made it back to the general store that afternoon. They had made their way into Cook County and were now heading toward the mountain to meet the soldiers who had been there for days buttressing the mountain. The energy was suddenly different again, with people pacing the general store and realizing that there was no way the battle was going to fade away. It was coming to their front door, and it would be there sooner than later.

Will's father stood behind the counter at the store with his brows furrowed deeply and his jaw set like he had a mission. Will leaned against the shelves and watched as his father rung out everyone's purchases, their buying even more frenzied than usual. They grabbed things from the shelves as they asked with wide eyes if everyone had heard that the Union had arrived.

"Where are the boys?" Will's mother's voice rang out as the door to the store opened.

"I'm right here, Ma," he said, looking at her and seeing panic on her face. "Where's Sam?"

"I left him at his house. We're okay, Ma. The Yankees haven't got us."

"You think it's funny. They're coming. You'll see. Tomorrow your father will be ringing out supplies for the boys from the north," she said, raising her voice and looking toward her husband for support.

"The boys are safe. Soldiers are soldiers and I'll ring them up the same," his father said, plainly.

Will knew his father had deeper feelings about the war, but the last few days of gossip and worry were draining and he looked like he was ready for the battle to be over, regardless of how it went.

WITHIN A FEW SHORT DAYS AND several confrontations, Union troops had started to trickle onto the street that held the General Store and the Barbershop. Their uniforms were different than the ones the townspeople were used to seeing, and their general demeanor was also different. They seemed foreign to everyone who was out and about when they arrived.

There was a different swagger to their steps, and they seemed louder. Their body odor was worse than mules that had been plowing all day, since most of them hadn't bathed in the last week or more. Will watched as two of them jostled each other on the porch of the store, looking like they were not much older than he was. He tried to listen to what they were saying to each other, but could only catch every other word or so. They seemed as certain that they would take the mountain as the Confederates were when they came through.

The women were worried that the arrival of the troops meant the battle might start right there, on the porch. Of course, that wasn't the case, but it didn't stop them from being extra cautious, and begging the boys not to stay far from their eyesight, lest they get wrapped up in the excitement and end up part of the war.

The northern soldiers came from all over the place, with some originating in New York and New England, while others had arrived from further west - places like Ohio, which seemed more like the locals to the boys than New York did. It took a moment, or two, but it became easy to see which soldiers came from where. Those from the East seemed harder. They had seen more battles and were more war worn, stretched thin from the travel and the fighting and the losses that they had already seen.

They walked down the street like they didn't see the civilians, never really making eye contact or speaking much. Some of the men in town would stare when they would walk by, but it was rare that the men in blue wool even noticed. When they did address the civilians, it was in short, choppy language that sounded more like barking than talking.

The men from Ohio, Indiana and Illinois were different—their accents sounded more familiar. Although they appeared to be less seasoned, they had an air of determination and focus that sent a shiver up your spine. Their walk and hands showed a ruggedness of people who meant to finish the job. They were younger, too, as Will noticed, with the bright smiles of youth. The war was still exciting for them, and some of them had not yet seen the bare bones of battle, only hearing what fighting was like from those who had been enlisted for a little longer. Their voices would carry down the road as they came. They talked excitedly amongst each other, occasionally even falling out of their soldier posture for a moment of ribbing or horse play. The whole world was new to them and being with the Union was letting them explore it. Most had never been off the farm until now.

As the day wore on, the rain fell more softly, and people became more brazen at coming out to watch the soldiers. Many of the people who lived in the tiny clapboard farmhouses that dotted the field and the road between Big Shanty and Marietta had gone and taken down their Confederate flags when the Union arrived, lowering them and stashing them in their homes, like they had hidden the cows and pigs in the days before. The idea was that nobody really wanted more trouble than would come along naturally with the cannons and the horses that were now a part of the local scenery.

Not everyone took that approach, and some of the men still hung the flag proudly from the fronts of their houses. Some of the other shop keepers had taken a similar route, allowing the flag to stay where it had always been, as though they were unaware of what was going on around them. The Union soldiers would snicker when they saw the flag, spitting on the ground underneath it and joking that the Confederacy was going to find itself under a new flag soon.

WILL KICKED OPEN THE DOOR TO the general store with his muddy boot. His hands were full of supplies his father had sent him for from the stock shed out back. As he entered the store, he realized that it was full of Union troops. Four of them wandered around the shelves, looking and pawing at the wares. He shuffled around the edge of the store, to the back counter, where he set down the things he had brought and looked up at his father.

Mr. Braunhoff stood as straight as an iron pole, his cool eyes tracing the steps of the men from the north. It wasn't that he didn't trust them, but rather that he knew conflict was on the tips of every man's tongue these days, and he didn't want to get involved. He looked over at his son and nodded somberly, acknowledging him. Will pulled up a stool and sat on it, watching his father watch the soldiers. They were whooping and hollering amongst themselves as they loaded their arms down with supplies for their camp.

One of the farmers that did regular business came in and saw that the store was full. For a moment, it looked like he was going to turn around and go back the way he had come, returning home without whatever it was that he needed. Braunhoff nodded at him and he stayed, closing the door behind him and stepping around the soldiers to the other side of the store. Will wondered what would happen if a Confederate soldier were to walk in now, and considered that the battle might start over the burlap sacks that lined the floor.

One of the soldiers stepped up to the counter and piled up the tins and boxes he had gathered. His hair was a dirty blonde that hung slightly over one eye. He had light skin and deep green eyes that stared at Mr. Braunhoff as he began to package the goods. Will wondered how old he was, and thought about practicing the kind of confident posture he had.

His father gave the soldier his total. The soldier reached into his waistband and pulled out a crumpled Union note, placing it on the counter in front of Braunhoff.

"We charge gold here," he said, eyeing the note and then the soldier.

"Do you now? Here in the South?" the soldier snickered, looking over at his friends before turning again to Braunhoff.

"Here in my store, yes. I charge gold. I don't know what these notes are worth," Braunhoff said, calmly. He didn't like the implication he was a southerner. He may have been more of a northerner than any of the men in uniform, but really, Braunhoff was a store owner. He didn't care about the war and would be happy when it was over and people stopped tearing up his shelves. Life had gotten crazy around him with every passing second that brought them closer to fighting.

"This Union note is a good currency, shop keep. And what's more, it's going to be the money of the land one day, soon," he said.

"You may be right. But that day hasn't come yet. And I still collect gold," Braunhoff said, nodding his head to affirm his point, and stepping forward toward the counter to show that he was not changing his mind any time soon.

The other soldiers had been standing there and watching silently, casting a glance amongst themselves every so often. They stepped closer to the counter now, shifting their eyes to Braunhoff and making it known that they backed up their friend on the subject of Union currency.

"Listen. I don't know who you think you are. But I am trying to pay for these here supplies from this ramshackle building you call a store. I'd think you would be happy to have money coming in at all, from the looks of it." The soldier leaned over the counter so he was staring Braunhoff in the face from just a few inches away.

"I'm not taking your money. It's paper. Gold is the only kind of money that flows through this shop, which was doing fine until you and your friends showed up. Now, if you don't have gold, I understand times are tough. But then, get out," Braunhoff snarled, pointing toward the door and narrowly jabbing the Yankee in the face with his finger.

Within moments, the store had devolved into a ransack. Will was unsure who had started it first, though he thought it was the tall soldier in the back, who had knocked over a sack of potatoes from the counter. The others joined in within moments, working quickly to topple the shelves and pull everything down to the floor. The store was a mess of flour and noise and Will got off his stool, but stayed in the corner and out of the melee.

His father was screaming now, jumping over the counter and into the middle of the fray. He hollered and hollered for the soldiers to leave, but they kept smashing shelves and glass jars. A few of them stepped next door the barber shop and turned it in the same way, spilling shaving cream over the floor and laughing as the lone customer bolted from the door to get away from what seemed like it might be the start of the war.

Sam's father was there after a moment, joining Braunhoff in yelling at the soldiers and telling them to return to their Yankee caves. Braunhoff reached out and grabbed one of the men by the shoulder as he was about to knock over the scale. The soldier wheeled around and punched Braunhoff in the jaw. He returned the favor, sending the soldier back against the shelf behind him. Soon everyone was on Braunhoff, tackling him to the ground in a pile of blue wool and dragging him to the door.

Will watched in horror as they stood him up and hit him in the face, screaming that they were going to arrest him for what he had done. The store lay in shambles at their feet, and a crowd had gathered outside to watch what was happening. Will sneaked out the back door and around the front of the store. They had dragged his father outside now, who was still scowling, even with a bruise showing up on his face in the gray light of day.

Tillet had become the voice of reason, brokering between Braunhoff and the Union soldiers, until he was able to get Braunhoff sent home for house arrest, instead of dragged off to the camp of the enemy. Braunhoff said nothing during the conversation, which was probably for the best. Will felt a certain relief that his father would be at home and not in jail, though he wondered how he would be fare being with his mother all day.

Sam's father took Braunhoff by the hand and led him down the road to their homes. The soldiers stood outside the store for a moment longer, laughing and jostling each other, proud of their force. The store was wrecked, and they stepped through the supplies to pick up their original wares, carrying them out the front door, this time without leaving even a paper note.

Will sat on the stoop and felt his stomach roll. The day had started out the way they all did lately—with rain falling on the roof and soggy shoes, but had turned so bad. He knew his father was going to be alright but he began to wonder about what was really going to happen when the fighting began.

He didn't have much time to think about it, because a thunderous boom rang through the forest and down the road. The ground shook beneath him and he was immediately on his feet. He looked around and saw that others had felt it and heard the commotion and were also looking to see if they could find where it came from. He scanned the road and looked back toward the train depot, but saw nothing but mud and rain. He grabbed the porch railing and lifted himself up, giving him a better vantage point.

Off in the distance, a plume of smoke broke through the tree line and rose, in a different shade of gray, up to the clouds. He watched it and felt his heart sink through the floor of his chest. The Lacey Hotel was burning.

Chapter Eleven

ON GOING EDUCATION

*O*badiah watched the troops from inside the door of his home. They paid him no mind, walking on down toward the general store, talking amongst each other. Everyone in town was nervous now that Federal troops were in and out of town in larger groups, but Obadiah felt particularly uneasy. The world outside his door was changing rapidly and it concerned him.

It had been a few days since the first slave wagons had come in, laden down with men shackled to one another, and the feeling that it brought back to Obadiah hadn't receded at all. Watching the wagons roll down the dirt street toward the sound of the mountain construction for the Confederate lines had reminded him how recently it had been that he had been in shackles himself.

Sometimes, it was easy to regret. It was never easy to remember. He sighed and watched the blonde men in blue uniforms continue on their way. He had run into them yesterday—he recognized the shorter one by the particular gait he had—like one leg was a hair longer than the other. They had been coming out of the general store when Obadiah was going in, and the soldier had glared at Obadiah and closed the door without holding it open. Obadiah had tried to pay it no mind, knowing that just because he had found a place to live that respected him as a free man didn't mean that everyone was going to feel the same way.

Since the Union soldiers had arrived, he had found it easier to just keep his distance. Most people were choosing to do that anyway, seeing that everyone was nervous about when the battle would start and nobody wanted to be there when it did. His wife had been keeping the children inside for the last few days, nervously watching them and staring out the front window.

Obadiah stepped out onto the porch and sat on the wooden chair that was next to the door. He sighed as he thought about what it had taken to be rid of his slave chains. For all the struggle he had seen, he was always aware that others had been in far worse situations than he had. Most of them never had the opportunity to earn their freedom, and he was thankful every day that he had been.

He wore the scars of his time on the plantation under his clothes, and there wasn't a day that passed that he didn't think about the time where he was free and working to buy the freedom of his family. That separation had worn on him, leaving its own scars, which ran deeper than those across his skin. There was nothing he valued more now than the ability to be home with his family—that they were free from the slave plantation was enough for him.

In the months after he and his family were free they traveled around trying to find a place where they could settle without enduring the dangers of being slaves in white America. They had traveled to Georgia from lower Alabama and managed to finally find a space to call their own—building a small house on a plot of land and setting up their first home. Obadiah had been an expert smith for the man who had owned him, and he opened a shop near the general store that stood in town.

The first weeks there brought about the occasional look from someone who was surprised to see a freed slave living there, but overall people seemed to mind their business more. Gradually, he made friends with some of the people who lived around there—like Braunhoff and Tillet and the others. It had been a comfort to have people that didn't look at him with the disdain he saw in the faces of most people over his life.

His son often ran around with their boys—playing in the woods or in the fields out behind the houses. Life had found some semblance of peace for his family, and the arrival of troops made him wonder how long that was going to last. He sighed and leaned back in his chair, looking out at the road. The rain had started yesterday, and today it seemed a little harder. The road was mud, and the grass in the yard was bent down from the force of the drops. He thought that it was fitting for the way things were shaping up around them.

As the troops came from the North, Obadiah realized he had to tread even more carefully. It was easy to assume that the soldiers from the south did not approve of a freed slave, but with the northerners it was harder. Some of them paid him no mind as he walked along the street. That wasn't always the case.

"Get off the road, damn you!" a voice hollered from behind him. He was walking down to the shop to try and get some work done. He stopped and turned, looking through the rain to see who was speaking. It was a union soldier. He was tall—six foot, with dark hair and bright, pale skin. He sneered at Obadiah.

"Excuse me?" Obadiah said, unsure of what he had heard.

"Get out of the road," he repeated, staring at Obadiah with disgusted glee.

Obadiah stepped off the road and stood in the grass, taking a few more steps back. The whole time, the soldier stood there, staring at him. Obadiah felt his heart speed up a pace, as he realized that the man might not be happy with him having simply left the road. The sound of the rain filled his ears as he watched the soldier glare at him, considering what to do next.

Finally, the soldier stepped forward and spit in Obadiah's face, before turning and walking on down the road toward town. Obadiah stood in the rain for a long while, not moving. He watched the figure get smaller and smaller, and looked around to see if there was more. He was all alone. He took a deep breath and stepped back up into the street, turning back toward his home.

A few paces later and he stopped again. This time, he turned back toward town and took a resolute step forward. He thought about what he had done for his freedom and how much he had already suffered. He wasn't going to spend every day locked in his house, worrying about whom he might meet in town, and he didn't want his wife to worry—and she would if he came home instead of going into town.

The mud squished under his shoes as he started back down the road for the second time that day. His heart had finally slowed down, but his head was racing. He had thought about the ways that incident earlier could have played out—he had felt trapped for the first time since he had cast off his shackles, and he knew that danger was going to be there as long as the soldiers were there.

The day before, he had been approached by a northern soldier who wasn't hostile. He sat down next to Obadiah by the general store and asked him if he was a freed slave.

"I am indeed, sir," Obadiah answered, nodding his head.

"How is that possible?" the soldier asked, sounding like it was beyond reason. "Ain't all Negroes slaves down here?"

"I was able to buy my freedom, sir," he answered. "My master was a good man."

"I see. He must have been. Most slaves never would be able to buy their freedom. Freedom wouldn't even be a word they knew," the soldier said.

"I know. I was very, very lucky. I had never expected he would offer me freedom."

"How long have you been freed now?"

"Oh, a number of years now. I built a house here a few years back," Obadiah smiled, feeling a little calmer after talking to him for a moment.

"You have your own house?" he asked, the surprise creeping back in his voice. Obadiah laughed. "Of course, I do. I bought my freedom and then I built my house," he replied.

Obadiah thought about that conversation as he got closer to town. His stomach was flipping as he started to scan the streets for the spitting soldier from before. There had been real anger in his eyes and Obadiah didn't want to have an incident if they ran into each other again by the general store. He didn't seem to be anywhere, so Obadiah took a deep breath and began to walk a little more relaxed.

He thought about how different his life was from that of the men down the road that had been brought in on wagons. They wouldn't have the opportunity to walk down the main street of town and step into a general store. Even with the hostility that was finding its way into the town lately, he knew that was just a little part of a much bigger problem.

He went to his shop and worked for a few hours, listening to the sound of the rain, which was also working to keep the soldiers far away. The walk home was quieter, with him only passing a group of folks that were headed out to the mountain to watch the preparations.

The family walked with a level of excitement—two parents and their adolescent son. Obadiah asked where they were headed and felt a wave of sickness when they told him. He didn't understand the desire to go and watch the preparations for what was sure to be a bloody war.

They were excited though, talking excitedly about what they heard about dragging cannons up the mountain side, and how many men they were using to get the job done. Obadiah thought about the slave wagons and nodded. He didn't think that was an accomplishment by any stretch.

"What if the battle starts?" he asked, mostly being facetious, hoping they might think twice about going to watch.

"Doubtful it's gonna start today. Look, it's raining!" the man said, putting his hand out to catch the drops and laughing. Obadiah shook his head.

"You never know," he said.

"No, you don't. But this is just a little fun. They're still dragging cannons up the side of the mountain. There's no fighting starting soon. Now's the time to go watch. And I bet you people do go up and watch when it gets bloodier," he laughed.

"You're probably right." Obadiah conceded that more people would probably make their way to watch the spectacle. The thought was just making him sick. He said goodbye to the family and kept on toward home.

He knew never to be surprised at how people behaved—the plantation had taught him that. But sometimes, he was still surprised. Today had been a day for that. The soldier's cold hatred was still hanging in his head, and then the careless way that the couple talking about traipsing up the mountain to watch slaves dig trenches and soldiers prepare to slaughter. Odd, though, they were working side by side, as if it was all natural.

He knew what kind of ugliness people were capable of, and he was sure there was going to be plenty of it on the mountain.

Chapter Twelve

ARMAGEDDON'S DOORSTEP

June 27th burst open with sunshine, but unbearably hot—the first in days. The morning seemed like any of the calm ones that had come before it—minute stacking against the one that came before it with quiet consistence. The air was heavy with the tensions that had been building for weeks now, but for a moment, one could almost forget that war was knocking at the door, and simply enjoy the beautiful peace of an early summer morning.

But battle didn't stop for a quiet morning, and the days of assembling and digging in had culminated in a mountain that was crisscrossed with the patterns of war and ready for action. The Confederates were eager to get the first shot—to show the Yankee scum that they weren't standing any northern antics and were ready to put up a fight for their mountain. The soldiers all shared the same resolute look on their young faces; the sunlight making it hard to see the fear in their eyes.

The first shot broke through the heavy summer air with instantaneous permanence, and the morning was split wide open. The shot met resistance in the water tower that sat at the base of the mountain. It penetrated the side of the vat with force and the sound of cracking and tearing that caused everyone to stop and listen. Within a second, water was pouring from the tower and down its legs to the dirt below. The rush of water sounded like the rain that had been falling on the ground for days, and from a certain angle it looked as though the tower were weeping.

The next shots rang out quickly across the mountain, ringing out through the trees. In between shots, the first hollers and screams could be heard. Whatever birds hadn't already left the mountain during preparation, scattered into the sky and fled. After the first rounds of shooting, cannon fire made its entrance. The mountain rumbled as the first iron ball came flying from its resting place, tearing through tree and men without discretion.

The houses in town shook and windows rattled with the thunder of the cannons. There was no mistaking it—the battle was here. After weeks of thinking about it, and preparing for it, and whispering about it behind closed doors, it was here. The General Store was empty—everyone was home that morning, hesitant to venture farther than their own four walls.

June 27, 1864

Dear Momma and Poppa,

I thought I'd write you a letter while I have some time to do so. We just ate breakfast and are getting orders. It's early and already getting hot!

Things are really heating up down here. We have the Rebels pushed back to a line of mountains and ridges not far from Atlanta. The largest are called Kenesaw and Little Kenesaw. General Sherman assures us we'll be in Atlanta in no time and then we can take a little rest and knock the dirt off. It sure is hot here and the bugs and flies bite like they're at a feast. The underbrush is no better. It's so thick and intertwined that it feels like you're wading through a wall of razors. I hadn't had a bath in sometime, but we don't notice the stink because we all smell the same. Boy, is dirt democratic, ha-ha! You'd laugh, Poppa, since we haven't had time, my beard has grown out and is about five inches long. Almost everybody has 'em.

Oh, I met a Negro man in one of the little towns close by the other day. He told me he was a freed slave and that he bought his freedom. After a while, he bought his family's freedom, too. He came here from Alabama, started a blacksmith shop and built a house. I am very happy for him, he seems to be a very considerate person. It will be great when all men can be free and have the opportunity to make a living for his self. That's one good thing that will come out of all this.

I find it hard to hate these people down here. They're a lot like us back home, mostly farmers and storekeepers. Many around these parts are even from Ohio some way or the other. They all came down to make a future when the railroad was being built to Chattanooga. I miss you, the family and the farm very much. How's old Karlo? Is he still chasing Mrs. Schmidt's cats? Give him a hug and a scratch behind the ear for me and tell 'em I'll bring him some good soup bones back for him to gnaw on.

We are on a ridge overlooking a small creek now. Over on the other side is a steep hill up to another ridge where the Johnny Reb's are dug in. We can see 'em when they peep over their battlements. There seen to be a lot of 'em. We will be going right into the heart of the whole mess. I'm not worried though. We have the best leading us. Colonel Dan McCook will be leading the advance and we have been assigned to his battalion. He's best friends with General Sherman and a very determined fellow. He's like old Karlo when he gets hold of a fox. He won't let go and shakes 'em until the life is drained out of their hides. They tell us a fellow by the name of Cheatham is holding the Reb's position, but Colonel Dan says we can whoop 'em and set 'em runnin'.

Well, we've just been ordered to pile our camp equipment and provisions. That's so we'll be free to maneuver better fightin'. We'll get 'em back after we're through givin' Johnny Reb a "Dutch Rubbin'." I sure can't wait to get back home and roll in that black Indiana soil. I plan not ever leaving it again.

Got 'a run, they're collecting our letters and we're starting to move.
Give my best to all and tell Katherine I said, "Hello!"

Your loving son,
August H. Greive

NOW THAT THE BATTLE HAD STARTED, nobody was sure how long it was going to go on for. Mrs. Braunhoff paced back and forth across the wooden floor in the kitchen, occasionally stopping by the window to look out into the yard. It was as though she was checking to make sure that the fighting was staying on the mountain. Will stayed home that morning, not daring to venture out because of how it would make his mother feel. He sat on the porch, where he could listen to the sounds of war better.

The cannons weren't so loud as they were thunderous, causing everything to rock when they fired off. Sometimes they were immediately followed with the sounds of trees crashing down to the ground, felled by the cannonball. Will pictured the way the trenches had been dug, where the cannons had been set up. He could imagine what the fighting might look like, having watched from the forest.

Finally, Will found a moment to escape his mother's watchful eye, and his father nodded approval. He took the opportunity to go out into the yard and head down the road into town. The air outside was heavy and smelled of smoke that rolled off the mountain. People were out and about now, congregating at the General Store and on the street. They pointed in the direction of the mountain with awe and fear on their faces, talking about what must be happening out there, and wondering how it was all going to end.

"I didn't think it would be this loud," a woman said, her voice high and hesitant, holding her hands over her ears.

"How long do you think it will go on?" someone else asked, looking around. Mr. Tillet looked over and saw Will, and nodded at him. "Sam is around here somewhere. I'm surprised your parents let you out," he said to Will.

"I am surprised, too, sir. Father gave me permission. Mother never would have let me out of the kitchen!"

"That's for sure," he laughed.

Suddenly, another salvo of rounds burst forth, causing another earthquake.

Instinctively everyone grabbed their ears and crouched close to the ground.

Will went off to look for Sam, wondering where he had gone off too. As he walked down the road, he passed a group of men and women going in the direction of the battle. One of them had a blanket thrown over his arm, like they were on a picnic. Will listened to them talking about going to watch the battle—curious to see what was causing all of the noise. They were almost cheery about the thought, which was a stark contrast from the people at the store who were worried about the edges of battle and safety blurring.

June 27, 1864

My Dearest Nell,

It's early morning and I have taken time to write you this letter.

I miss you with every passing minute I am any distance from you. Your absence makes the days longer with each passing moment. We're mostly busy during the day with keeping our eyes on the enemy and constant maneuvering, which changes every time we seem to be into position and can grab a minutes rest. Your Father is constantly on the move. He never seems to take a moment for himself, however he loves all this and takes to it as a natural. The men practically worship him and admire his bravado.

I said the days grow longer the more we're apart, but the nights, oh the nights, they are the torture that's the most unbearable. After we retire and extinguish our lights, I lie in my cot and have a horrible time trying to sleep. You enter my thoughts as a vapor moves through the trees. I see your lovely face and the sparkle in your eyes as you look upon me. Your smile enables me to forget all I see and do in this terrible confrontation. My heart races and I imagine I'm running my fingers ever so lightly though your soft flowing hair. The warmth of your cheek against mine and you sweet gentle kiss upon my brow is so real that I can hardly stand it. The other men don't see the tears that stream down my cheeks as I think of you, but somehow I feel they too are going through the same anguish as I.

Someday, soon we all hope, this blasted war will come to a conclusion and we can all be reunited with our loved ones back home. Then, my Dearest Loving Dove, we will stroll, arms locked close in lovers embrace, through the rose garden behind your parents' house as we did before. The fragrances of the blossoms trying in earnest to distract us from each other's gaze on a warm summer's night. To feel you close to me, holding me, kissing, is all I live for. Without you, my Darling, life would be a hollow existence.

We are preparing to strike at the Reb's as I write. Your Father has informed me we are assigned to Col. Dan McCook and the 85th Illinois. We're to lead the assault on a General Cheatham. Although they say he's a formidable leader, we have the best in McCook on our side. He's a go get 'em man and after he met with your father and the other company commanders, your father was as excited as a little school boy.

Think of me always by your side while I'm gone and cherish the day we'll be reunited, never parting again. I promise to be home soon.

Hold this parchment close to your soft lips as it holds my kisses!

With My Eternal Love,
Robert

Will walked down the road for a long while, right behind the first row of trees. The spectators had cut across a while back, trying to get as close as possible. He knew better than that and worked to put more distance between him and the fighting. Finally, he crossed the dirt road and began to make his way a little ways up the mountain. He didn't want to go high enough to get stuck needing to get down quickly. He wanted to keep the road in his sights—there would be no use in getting in trouble by the battle, or worse.

He couldn't hear the sounds of the forest through the crashing of the fight. The air was thick with screaming and the sound of cannon fire, and the cracking of bullets. As he got closer, it got louder and it felt like his whole head was rumbling along with the forest floor. The air got thicker with smoke and it burned the back of his throat as he breathed.

Amongst the cannons and gunfire there was a new sound— Will's heart. It was beating louder in his chest as he got closer to the battle. He still couldn't see anything, but he knew the mountain and knew he was dangerously close to stumbling upon the outer edge of the battlefield. He slowed down and hung back a little, suddenly second guessing his decision to come out into the woods to get a closer look. He stopped and leaned against a tree for a moment to take a breath and consider how much farther he wanted to go.

There was a crashing of branches to his right and his heart jumped. He got down and pressed himself against the tree as the crash continued. He couldn't make out what it was, but knew it was close and getting closer. Branches cracked and fell to the ground and there was the sound of dirt being kicked up by hooves. It was a horse.

Suddenly, Will could see the horse from where he was hiding. It was a dark animal and its mane was flying. Its eyes were wild and Will could tell it was scared. It clamored with the sound of its saddle and reins. Through the leaves, Will could see a soldier in the seat, his torso dark with sweat or blood. Will held his breath as the horse came closer. They broke through the trees and were a few feet from Will, giving him full view of the animal and its rider.

Will wanted to vomit, gagging. He wanted to scream, too, but his throat would cooperate with neither command. All he could do was sit there, dizzy with disgust, as looked at the torso of the soldier, which Will could now see was slumped over to one side, its arms lifelessly holding onto the reins. The grey fabric of the uniform was drenched in blood and ragged at the neck, where flesh and bone and wool all jutted toward the sky, absent the head that would normally have been there.

The horse raced by, the headless form bobbing with each step past Will as he watched with horror and fear. He watched for a long time as the horse tore through the woods. The sound of hooves stayed in his ears long after they had faded from the forest, and every time he closed his eyes, he saw the blood soaked uniform and chunks of flesh at the shoulder, bouncing as though a ghost were going off to battle. He vomited in the dirt next to him, violently trembling as a spontaneous torrent of tears cascaded over his flushed cheeks.

Finally, he pulled himself to his feet and steadied himself against the tree that had hidden him. He took a step forward, and another, in the direction he had come. The sound of the battle raged behind him as he started home. His steps quickened, and soon he was running through the trees without any care for being heard. The only thing he wanted was to get as far away from the fighting as possible. He took deep, heaving breaths that filled his lungs with air as he pounded his feet into the ground, scrambling falling and stumbling, down the base of the mountain and back across the road. He turned and headed for town, not looking back once.

He burst into his house, slamming the door closed behind him. His mother stared at his face before rushing over and wrapping him in her arms. His father came in from the next room and stood in the doorway, watching his wife embrace Will. Will looked over his mother's shoulder at his father, whose eyes were heavy and serious.

Will couldn't talk about what he saw, barely nodding his head when his mother asked if he had seen something. She didn't press him, not wanting to upset him more than he obviously was. It took a long time for his breathing to slow down to normal, and his eyes were full of terror that didn't fade.

Shaking and wild-eyed, all he could blurt out was "Gone... gone...nothing there!" Then with another explosion of tears, "His head...gone!"

He sat at the table that night without eating.

June 27, 1864
Big Shanty, Georgia

Dear Eleonore,

We have been extremely busy here in Georgia. It sure is nothing like our home country in Illinois. It's hot, dirty and the scarcity of refinements defines this God forsaken place as having a total lack of civilization. The further we progress, the more my disrespect for these "Seccesh Scoundrels" grows, bordering on the line of total hatred. If wasn't for being such a good Christian in our area, I'd hate them completely, absolutely and pray to our God above for their total annihilation!

We are keeping busy and I will admit to you, and you only, these Rebs are a stubborn lot. Although we keep pushing them back toward Atlanta, they hold firm and even come right at us. Blasted Fools! We're past a place called Big Shanty located on the railroad to Atlanta among a series of ridges that run off the mountain here called Kenesaw. Burnt the railroad inn there to show the locals our power and that we won't stand for any loyalty to the South.

The Rebs have dug in on the high ground and have secured the mountain. We shouldn't have any trouble dislodging them though. If they do like they have been doing, they'll fight a little to protect the remainder of their army and then retreat. We have them far outnumbered and our stores and munitions are coming down from Chattanooga via the railroad we rebuilt. There is no way we can't just push them out like a tidal wave. We are far more superior and Sherman shows no mercy.

We're in an area now located south of the railroad and the mountain. We can see the Rebs' lines across a little creek along a ridge. They appear to be well dug in, but we're to attack straight at them, it's called a Frontal Attack. It should be exciting! This morning we officers were called together before sunrise. Brigadier General Davis placed us under Colonel Dan McCook in the Third Division. I feel good being with him since he comes from a long line, the famous "Fighting McCook's." He's a handsome young fellow, but has a strong will and determination that will guarantee us victory.

He and I have talked in the evenings about our law careers and what we plan doing after the defeat of the Secessionists. He was a law partner with Sherman you know and has great political connections. I shared with him our plans for the Illinois Governorship and he's assured me he can get General Sherman's endorsement. I will be close to him in the attack and should obtain plenty of exposure. I should come out of this a hero with McCook. Think of it Eleonore, what with my record of battle, Sherman's endorsement along with the power of the Boys in Springfield and a Daguerreotype of Lincoln pinning a medal on me, there is no way in this world I shouldn't be Governor.

It was tremendous to hear that Kenneth has returned home. He's a strong intelligent lad and will be a great asset to the law firm. It's too bad he has a game leg after being shot, but he should be able to gain a lot of support with it when he's my campaign manager in our county. No doubt all the girls will moon over him and don't forget, their fathers' vote.

Robert keeps talking about Nell when we are in camp. I think everyone in the whole Union Army has seen her picture and knows who she is. I know the separation is harsh on young lovers, but we old hounds have come accustomed to that sort of thing. I feel after today, we will be coming home to the two of you very soon. I'll stop on the way home and bring you a new dress for the many parties you'll be hosting before the election. I'll make sure it's a blue one to match your eyes with plenty of ribbons and lace.

I have to go now, since they are collecting our letters before we line up. Remember, I love you.

Your Loving Husband,
Captain James Oliver Wilkerson

SAM SAT NEXT TO WILL ON the porch, staring off down the road in the direction of the battle. He had a ton of questions for his friend, but knew that Will didn't want to talk about what he had seen. It seemed to Sam that most of the folks who had gone out to the mountain came back and didn't really want to talk about what happened. He had watched a man stop a group of young women from going down the road, shaking his head and waving them back.

He had heard some stories though, sitting on the porch of the store. Folks said the bodies were piled up like logs, or scattered across the field. They said the air was heavy with smoke and the smell of blood, which seemed to be everywhere. Nobody described the scene with excitement, but instead with quiet, serious voices. It wasn't what everyone had expected.

All the days spent talking about what it would be like—how soldiers would file across the battlefield and fight, and how the mountain was being armed— nothing touched the reality of the fighting. Those who ventured through the woods to the edge of the fighting were met with a mountainside of men dying around them. Gunshots and cannonballs took down men with ease, bringing them to their final resting place in the thick, wet mud. The trenches that had been carved by man were now carved too by fallen trees and cannonballs and filled with bodies, now weaponless as their guns got handed off to the next body that needed them.

Chapter Thirteen

REALITY'S DREAM

The battle raged on with fury. The mountain sounded like it was coming down around the village, and nobody was really sure that wasn't the case. Will had run through the woods and straight home, where he collapsed in a sobbing heap and let his mother hold him close. He couldn't tell what he had seen, but he didn't really need to say anything. She could tell. His father came over and held him too, stroking his hair like he was a small child. The air was somber. Will finally pulled away from his parents and went to sit on the stairs inside, staring off into the air in front of him without saying a word.

On the battlefield, guns and cannons rang out through what remained of the forest around them. Trees were destroyed by bullets and iron balls, and screams echoed over the sound of the fighting. The troops were right on each other, guns barrel to barrel across the trenches. Soldiers on both sides stepped over bodies as they made their way to the front, picking up supplies they might need as they marched into the melee.

Sherman had brought his troops around the flank and surprised the others. It had been an unexpected move and the battle showed that evidence everywhere. The carnage poured from the mountain side onto the road by the rail station. The town itself was spared by the violence, but rampaged for supplies in the final minutes of fighting. Union troops carried things they found back up the mountain as they made a last attempt to dig in and fight the Confederate soldiers.

The bodies piled up as the battle wore on and wound down. Trees limbs and soldiers were piled on top of each other in grotesque statues along the battlefield. Uniforms and abandoned weapons littered the ground. At the bloodiest engagement, the leader of the Union soldiers was Colonel Daniel McCook. He was a personal friend of Sherman's and one of the first to fall. He shouted gallantly to his men leading the charge. As he mounted the Confederate ramparts, he was instantly shot point blank, falling forward toward the Confederate trenches before him. A hand grabbed him from behind and his soldiers pulled him back across the ground so that he might at least have the dignity to die on his own side of the battle. Dying was everywhere. The soldiers were faced with it and tripped over it with every step as they approached their own end. Screams competed with the sound of cannons and falling trees as the chaos rolled on.

WHEN THE BATTLE WAS FINALLY OVER, there was nothing living left on the mountain. The ground was piled high with bodies and debris. The tall Georgia Pines that had once filled the entire area were felled or splintered. Their ragged forms jutted from the ground toward the sky as if calling for help from someone who didn't answer in time. The face on the bodies looked much the same.

The air was filled with the heavy smoke that still lingered from the cannon blasts and bullets that rained down on the bodies and scarred the land. The smoke and stench sifted off the mountain and across the road, into the surrounding area. People could smell it from town–the acrid, sickly scent of war that now seemed to hang on the air everywhere.

It was a while before the people finally began to venture from their homes to look at what was left. The general store had been wiped clean. The windows were broken and the shelves were bare, nearly every supply pulled from the shelves and taken. The ground was covered in litter and dust and broken window bits. Will stepped carefully as he followed his parents around the small building. Nothing much had been spared in the area, and they weren't the only ones with broken windows. Everyone could be seen surveying the damage. Women held their hands to their mouths, and shook their heads softly. The men gathered on the porch of the general store and started to talk about what they needed to do next. Their voices were even and heavy with the weight of what was going on around them. There was shock in everyone's eyes. Even the preparations and the discussions in the days before the battle started couldn't prepare them for what had actually happened.

Slowly, they started to pick things up. Sam's father began to sweep out the general store, sending glass and dust out onto the porch and into the dirt. A breeze came in through the broken windows, bringing with it the faint scent of rot. He wrinkled his nose and kept sweeping, trying not be bothered by it. Someone had even removed the doors of the shop, which he now noticed, walking over to inspect the bent hinges. It was destruction everywhere.

Obadiah's shop had been ransacked as well, and all of his smithing tools taken. There had been two mules in the shed, waiting for shoes, and he had considered hiding them, like some of the folks did. He had decided not to, after talking to their owner, and left them in the barn. They were now gone, and their pen destroyed. He pounded his fist against the wall of the shop and looked around. It would take time to rebuild everything. Everyone was coming to the same conclusion as he was. He went and sat down on the stoop, unsure of where to start.

Will and Sam and Isaiah sat behind the general store in the dirt. Will was still nearly silent, and his eyes looked frightened and sad.

"Let's go see," Sam said. He nodded his head in the direction of the mountain behind them.

"I'm not so sure," Isaiah said, looking at Will.

Will wasn't paying attention.

"I want to see. You do too. Will does, too, right?" Sam asked, looking at Will.

Will nodded halfheartedly and kicked the dirt.

"Alright, fine," Isaiah gave in and stood up.

Sam and Will followed suit and they headed down the road toward the station. None of the adults were paying any attention to where they were going—they were too wrapped up in cleaning up the rubble that had been their town. As the boys walked down the road, they came across one or two other folks who had gotten the same idea. They joined up and kept heading in the direction of the depot and the mountainside.

The depot was all but gone completely. The train tracks remained across the ground, but the platform and outbuildings were splintered and torn by cannons and devastation. There was smoke drifting over the trees, which cast everything in an eerie, grey haze. Sam shivered a bit as they stepped slowly up the slope of the mountain, around the depot.

Bodies were everywhere. Some of them had been buried in shallow graves, with dirt piled over them lightly. Uniform bits still stuck out and caught the sunlight, when it shifted through the smoke.

In the hours since the soldiers had left, animals had begun to return. They too wore tiny looks of disbelief as they tried to recognize what had been their home. Some of them had found the shallow graves and pulled the bodies from them, finding sustenance in the remains and chewing on them with abandon. Other bodies weren't buried, but simply laid out bloated in the heavy air. The boys all held their breath. Trees were down everywhere, and made the battlefield look even more dangerous. Bodies slumped over logs. Others lay crushed under them, innards and bone smashed into the dirt under the weight.

Will began to shake. His hands were clammy and he felt like he couldn't breathe. Sam and Isaiah tried to steady him, taking him by the shoulders and whispering. He couldn't be calmed though.

He stared at the puffy faces and blood stained ground and thought about the headless rider that had come tearing out of the woods at him. He felt the scream boiling in his throat again and he fought the grip of his friends.

The scent in the air was the worst thing the boys had ever smelled. At first it was shocking and sweet and then it caused them to gag as they tried to get any bit of breath that might be a relief of it. Sam let go of Will long enough to lean over and vomit on to the ground beside him. He stood back up and saw Isaiah was taking a similar course of action. The scent was sickly sweet and permeated everything. It rose from the blackened bodies and assaulted the boys as they reached for handkerchiefs to cover their faces.

Will was still, and then burst out laughing. He was crying, too, with tears rolling down his cheeks as he cackled. The other boys looked at him and then at each other and realized they need to leave. They turned Will around and tried to lead him away, but he struggled. He stood there laughing louder and louder before finally quieting into a pattern of soft sobs. He relented to his friends cajoling and finally began to trample out of the woods toward home.

NELL AND HER MOTHER SAT IN the parlor, enjoying the sunlight. The men would be returning soon, and they were excited. They had missed their soldiers something awful and anxiously awaited for them to return. Nell was excited about her engagement and the wedding that would be coming up. She had spent the last few weeks telling her mother excitedly about how she wanted a big house on the edge of town.

"I want to have three—no, maybe four, children. They'll look like Robert and I and they will be so sweet," she cooed.

"You are very excited," her mother chuckled.

"I am. I've missed Robert and I can't wait to be married to him!" She clapped her hands in front of her and giggled, her eyes lighting up the same way they had since she was a child.

Suddenly, there was a knock at the door. Nell jumped up to answer it as her mother jokingly chided her to slow down.

"Young ladies don't hurry. It's undignified!" she exclaimed.

Nell just looked over her shoulder and laughed as she pulled the doorknob open. In front of her stood Mr. Hastings, the telegrapher from the Illinois Central depot down the street.

"Another telegram!" Nell called over to her mother, smiling at Mr. Hastings. Mr. Hastings handed her telegram without a word and turned to go back down the steps. Nell thought it was strange that he didn't want to chat. He was always the type that had something to say and took the time to say. She shrugged her shoulders and closed the door, looking at the yellow telegraph paper.

"Who is it from?" her mother called.

"Probably another RSVP," she laughed, "but I hope it's from Robert!" Nell's mother listened for a minute and didn't hear anything.

"Nell, don't be so secretive. Give a share!" Nell's mother joked as she rose from the divan across the parlor. As she reached the door, she saw Nell repose against the door, her eyes staring straight ahead as if beholding nothing before her, the usually soft skin of her face as pale as a corpse and her body trembling as if it was mid-January instead of a hot Illinois summer. "What is it, Nell? Tell Mother."

Suddenly, Nell burst forward and ran through the house and out the back door, holding the yellow parchment close to her bosom, emanating a shriek resembling that of a Banshee, boiling up from the inner bowels of her dear soul. Her journey carried her through the well-manicured yard into the rose garden she and Robert called the lovers' rendezvous. The neighbors streamed out of their homes to wonderment of all the commotion. Nell collapsed in the garden next to the fountain where a statue of cupid, spewed forth water. She curled up around herself into a ball of human grief, her sobs echoing over the sound of the fountain and into the air.

Her mother stood at the back door and stared at her daughter. She didn't need to ask to know what the telegram had said. She wanted to help her daughter, but she was in shock herself. All she could do was stand there and watch. A maid approached her and tapped her on the shoulder.

"Excuse me," the maid said softly.

Nell's mother turned to face her. "Yes?" her mother asked.

"The Reverend Jackson is here to see you," the maid said, pointing in the direction of the parlor. "Should I send him out?" She looked over at Nell.

"I'll see him. Show him to the parlor." She hesitated and then slowly turned away to meet the reverend, looking back as she walked. Entering the parlor, Reverend Jackson stood, a grim look upon his usually smiling face.

"Please be seated, Reverend Jackson. What can I do for you?"

The reverend leaned forward and gently took Mrs. Wilkerson's hand. "I don't mean to be familiar, but what I have to tell you, you need to be strong."

"Is it about James?"

"Yes, he didn't make it. It was in Georgia, north of Atlanta," he said with a whimper in his voice and tears streaming down his face.

Nell's Mother slowly turned her head to the back of the house. She then understood. She stared as she, the reverend, and the neighborhood were serenaded by the dirge of grief.

The sun streamed through the parlor widow, and the fresh flowers kept giving forth their sweet fragrance, even in the sorrow.

Nell's mother rose from the parlor and left the Reverend where he sat. She wandered to the backdoor and out into the yard, taking slow steps over to her daughter. She sat down next to her and gathered her crying child into her skirt, trying to hold her to comfort her, but needing comfort too. She felt herself sobbing as she held Nell, clutching her tighter and tighter, as though they might lose each other too.

THE HEAT WAS OPPRESSIVE AS MR. Greive and his sons worked in the corn field. Since the war, the price of grain—particularly oats and corn—had gone up. The yield was going to be particularly good this year. 1864 had been a heck of a year at the farm, outside Aggie being away at war.

"Why did he have to go?" Auggie's father thought. "It started in the East and is funded by eastern bankers and southern plantation owners. There's a lot of truth in that saying 'rich man's war; poor man's battle.'" He continued to toil under the furnace above him. He sighed, knowing his son knew what he was doing, and that he would be home soon. He had been able to read the homesickness between the lines of his son's last letters. They would have a good harvest, and soon the family would be reunited and things would return to normal again.

Auggie's Momma was sewing on the front porch, watching the occasional wagon or person traverse the dirt road in front of their house. She enjoyed the shade and breeze, greeting passersby and getting the latest gossip. The cicada sang out their oscillating song, reassuring everyone this was truly summer. The ever-present insects' cadence mixed with the heat of the day made Mrs. Greive nod off and on.

Just as her chin rested on her chest, the sound of wheels coming into the barn yard caused her to sit up with a start, her sewing kit cascading onto the porch floor. It was her brother, Hermann, and his wife, Gerta. She stood and waved as they dismounted from their buggy and strode across the yard to her. The looks on their faces were not happy as they approached.

"Helga, vere ist Frederick?" inquired Hermann.

"I don't know. Vat ist it?" Helga looked at her brother and then turned toward the field where her Husband had been working.

"Jaust git Frederick!" he said straightforwardly.

Gerta stood by her husband and couldn't make eye contact with Helga. She felt her stomach fall as she realized that they had come with some sort of bad news.

"He stopped by the smokehouse to check on the hams," said one of the boys as they were returning from the field. "I'll fetch 'em!" He turned and ran back in the direction of the smokehouse. Helga felt herself shaking.

As Fredrick approached, Hermann grabbed him and hugged him close. Gerta went over to stand by Helga, putting her arm around her shoulder.

"It ist our Auggie. I vas down at der railroad station ven die telegram came! He ist gone!" he almost shouted in hysteria. He held his brother-in-law close to him.

Frederick stared in his face for what seemed hours, then blurted out, "Liar, you are a damned liar!"

He smacked Hermann squarely across the left cheek. Hermann hung his head and wept, and Frederick, trembling, did the same. They embraced each other and cried. Helga, hearing the news and witnessing the spectacle, dropped into her chair and pitifully looked up at Gerta. She had no words at first, her mind racing to capture what she was thinking. The only thing was a feeling of loss that sucked the air from her body.

"Yah, yah, ist true vat is said," burbled Gerta as she knelt down next to Helga, trying to give comfort.

The children ran to their mother and surrounded her with hugs. Suddenly, the mass of children and women broke into a mournful wail. Frederick broke away. Turning, he walked back toward the field. Hermann started to follow him, then stopped.

"He needs his own time now," he said to no one in particular. He watched his brother-in-law as he wandered off, becoming a tiny silhouette against a sky so blue you never would have known anyone could be mourning beneath it.

Frederick Greive wandered through the corn field, lost in thought. All he could say in a low voice was "Damn, damn." Stopping at the edge of the field he lifted his soaked face and cried out, "God, oh God, how could you do dis to me? My Auggie, my darling Auggie?"

He sat down and looked out over the farmland. He thought about his family. He thought about how they had come here to set up a life where they would be safe and happy. He had let his son go traipsing into war and now he would never be coming home. He felt the tears coming again, rolling over the salt that the last ones had left. He wiped his face and sighed.

Instinctively, he had wandered to the spot overlooking the O & M Railroad where he and Auggie would watch trains. They would always go there after chores were finished and made a game of where the trains were taking their passengers or what goods they were carrying. About that moment, the shrill whistle of a locomotive broke his thought. It was a troop train loaded with cannon, material, and solders going to the front in the east. On the platform of the last car were a couple of officers enjoying the fresh air and smoking cigars as they joked and laughed.

They had no idea what they were getting into. The only thing they could see were the shiny buttons on their uniforms and the patriotism that they had come to take as truth. He watched them as they leaned against the rail and pointed at the trees. Their voices carried up with so much happiness and optimism that ripped his heart open all over again. He remembered Auggie boarding the train, and leaving in a rush of excitement. He wanted to vomit, but instead pulled himself to his feet.

Frederick ran full speed down the hill to the railroad tracks. Running behind the ever receding train, he picked up rocks and threw them repeatedly at the men. They looked at him with shock as the train moved away, unsure of what was going on and why a man was chasing them down, hurling stones through the air.

Frederick kept running, picking up rocks and throwing them as hard as he could as though he might be able to change something if he threw one just hard enough to make contact. He was exhausted, and his lungs felt like they were going to explode from breathing and screaming.

"Damn you! Damn you! You have killed my little Auggie! May you all rot in Hell!" Frederick cried out.

As the train disappeared, Frederick exhausted, fell to his knees, crying in the dirt.

Chapter Fourteen

HOMECOMING

Auggie's body was buried on the hill behind the house, under a tree that swayed in the summer's breeze. The hill looked out over the wide fields that rolled on until they hit the line of tall trees at the edge of the farm. The sun set each day behind those trees, and Auggie's father had sat on that very spot with his son and watched the sky fade from blue to pink to purple before finally going dark. Frederick still went out at the end of a day in the fields. Over the years, his wife and eldest son thought he would go out there less. They did, and soon Auggie's brother had moved onto his own farm, and rarely sat on the hill anymore to be close to his brother. Their father still finished dinner every night and trekked out across the yard, his bones now heavy with age on top of sorrow.

There were nights when he stood there, under the tree, next to where his son lay, and thought back to the day when they loaded him on the train and sent him on his way with well wishes. He wished he could have gone back and fought harder for Auggie to stay put, but knew in his heart that his son would have gotten onboard anyway. All he wanted to do was fight to protect the country that his family had felt made a better home than where they had come from.

His wife had cried for months after the news came, and then she settled into a quiet acceptance. It bothered him sometimes how easily life had returned to something like normal after Auggie was gone. He had already been off the farm for a while, and so his absence felt like a dream for a long time—like he might be coming home at the end of the war. After a while, Frederick and his wife stopped talking about Auggie. They settled into a silent remembering between them, with Frederick making his trip to the hill on most evenings.

He watched his younger son when he came to visit with his new wife and young children, and thought about what Auggie would be like as an adult. It made him sad at times, and happy too, to imagine the man he might have become. Over the years, he whispered how proud he was of the man he *had* become, listening to it fade into the wind without response.

His wife sat by the fire in the farmhouse, rocking slowly in her chair. She listened to the sound of her husband's voice; singing German hymns into the night, still punctuated by occasional sobs after all this time. She had stopped joining him outside many years ago, choosing instead to mourn nightly from the fire, alone with her memories and calmed by the sound of her husband.

Obadiah sat on the front porch and looked out down the road. In the years since the war, more and more homes had cropped up. It had taken years after the last bullet before the mountain began to hide its scars, and anyone who wasn't a passerby could still see the wounds and injuries from one side of town to the next. Obadiah thought back to the first days after the battle had ended.

People had been shocked at first, as though they were all under some sort of spell. They walked around dazed for a few days, treading over the remains of the general store and other businesses. They looked at broken fences and for missing animals. The women huddled together in the safety of the church, which was missing a wall, but still had the Lord's protection. Everyone whispered. The children seemed to go from crying to giggling and back again at a rapid rate, unsure of how they should feel, and afraid of their own parents' current states. The air had felt nervous for weeks, like the fighting might start again. Like the nightmare might not be over.

Obadiah's shop had been ransacked and nearly destroyed. For a while he thought about leaving it as it was. Everyone talked of rebuilding, but some part of him was ready to move on, to something fresh. The mountain had the stench of death around it, and the town felt like it had been turned on its head. Rebuilding would take time and would be over old wounds. He was already aware that wounds like that never really healed.

For the first month, he left the shop in near disarray. The fact was that most people needed help rebuilding their businesses, and their homes, and he felt that was more important. Most people who might need his services in the first few days had a bigger problem on their hands—their horses and animals had been taken or run off. Isaiah had helped clean up the mess in the first few days, and then followed his father as he went around helping others.

Obadiah knew destruction. He knew what it meant to start over, and he recognized that feeling in the eyes of the folks he had come to know in town. He went down to the general store, which had sustained some of the most damage, and got to work picking through the rubble with Mr. Braunhoff and Tillet.

It was nearly a year before the main road looked like it had before the soldiers came, but like the mountain, still wore scars if you knew where to look. A number of people had packed their families and their possessions and left, not wanting to stay in the shadow of a mountain that had brought so many calamities. Those that chose to stay watched as their friends and family loaded up and headed out, trying to find a quiet spot where they might enjoy life and not think about war.

Obadiah's wife had considered it, herself, bringing it up at dinner one night. Obadiah had said that they would stay–that they should stay. They had already done more running than he cared to remember, and he could still see the happiness of home around him. Gradually, she came around, and felt like her husband did. Soon, she was the one encouraging him to take time from helping everyone else to rebuild himself.

Looking back, as he sat on the porch and watched the wind blow through the trees, he realized that the first year after the battle had been the easiest—in some ways. Kennesaw, and the country, were different after the war. People were broken, and shaken, and the countryside bore the scars that the families of those lost tried to forget. Gradually, people moved into the houses that had been left by those who wanted to get away, and new houses were built.

With new people came new opinions, and it was obvious very quickly to Obadiah that the years since the war had made the reasoning a little foggy. The word "reconstruction" sounded like "rebuild"—everyone putting their country back together, but other people saw it differently. There was no reason to rebuild or reconstruct, if something hadn't been destroyed in the first place. And the country had been destroyed.

Obadiah heard it in passing some days, when a farmer or man at the general store would make a remark about all that country had done to "free the blacks," as though the cost of that far outweighed the result. Obadiah had heard things worse than that, and tried to never let it crack him.

Isaiah was fierier, and would argue when he heard that, if he thought he could get a word in. Obadiah had been home one night when he son crept in the door with a black eye and a story to tell. He tried to remind his son that he knew where they had come from and they should be thankful enough to have made it as far as they had.

His son wanted more, as sons often do. Obadiah pressed him to study in school as much as he could, often not allowing him out until his work was done. By the time Isaiah was a young man, and ready to embark on his own life, he had been placing at the top of his class and been accepted to college.

College, which was completely foreign to Obadiah and his wife, was exactly what Isaiah needed. He wrote his parents letters that detailed how pleasant his classmates were, and how rigorous the work. Each note sounded happy, and Obadiah could sense his son growing up in the pages. He knew he would be okay.

In the months after her husband and future son-in-law fell on the battlefield, Mrs. Wilkerson focused almost entirely on Nell. The house filled with flowers and food immediately, as neighbors, lawmakers, and churchgoers all filed through the house to pay their respects. Nell kept herself locked in her room for the first few days, her sobs echoing through the door and down the hall. Her mother was more composed, crying only in her bed at night, after turning down the lamp.

The day of the funeral, Mrs. Wilkerson dragged Nell out of bed and dressed her, moving her like a life size ragdoll. Grief had aged her so much in such short time, and she looked much older than her sixteen years. Nell made it down the stairs, but slowed at the door. She shook her head and moaned, digging her heels into the ground, until her mother called for someone to help carry her outside. She wailed.

The crying eventually faded, and every so often, Nell would let out a smile that reminded her mother of what their life had been before the war happened, as she walked around her home, and her town, there were no signs of war, or battle. It would be easy to forget if the letters still didn't sit on the desk at home, with their words of war, and sorrow, and finally—loss.

She pushed her daughter to get out and be around people. She knew that Nell needed to be distracted, and to find joy in life again. It was an errand that never paid off, and Nell often went out to come back home immediately and lock herself in her room on the fourth floor. Her heart seemed to break every day, and after a while even her mother came to accept that this was simply how it was going to be, for a while.

But Nell stayed in her room for years. She would venture out with her mother, but besides that, came home and stayed there. At night, she paced the floor in her room, looking out the window into the moonlight and thinking about her lost love as if he would be looking up at her lovingly from the garden below.

Mrs. Wilkerson continued to go to church, and found herself out more after a while. Nell could take care of herself and Mrs. Wilkerson knew that she had a very real responsibility to keep the house and the finances in order. Her husband had always appreciated her intellect and capable nature, and Mrs. Wilkerson put that to her advantage in the years after her husband's death.

One day, almost three years after the news came about her husband, Mrs. Wilkerson met a man at church who had lost his wife. She could see the edges of pain still in his eyes, and offered to bring over some tea. He was appreciative, and told her that he would look forward to that. She went home that afternoon and prepared some tea and a package of cookies and set out to the other side of town.

She laughed that night like she hadn't in years. There was something about shared grief that brought people together. She felt like she could relax around him– she didn't need to pretend to be strong or unaffected. They could share the experience of losing one they loved, and the empty days that follow. It was nice to realize she wasn't as alone as she thought.

Tea and cookies became a regular occurrence for the two, and they married within in the year. Nell had tried to be happy for her mother, smiling when she shared the news over dinner one night, but it quickly faded to the sullenness that she had come to know. It wasn't that she wasn't happy for her mother, it was just impossible not to think of Robert, and how he would never be coming home.

Nell kept to herself; even after her mother married and they were all living together. She thought her mother's new husband was nice enough, but she was still fragile. Mrs. Wilkerson tried to get her help from as far away as Chicago, but doctors and specialists all said the same thing—she had a broken heart, and a fragile disposition, and those two things meant that she was struggling and probably would, maybe forever.

At first the news made her sad for her daughter. She wanted Nell to be the happy, laughing girl she was that day on the parade field so many years ago. But she was as dead as Robert was, and Mrs. Wilkerson knew that too. Nell grew pale and thinner than she had been, as though she was a living ghost. And she was.

When Robert was still alive, Nell had spent all of her free time in the nights reading his letters. The love poems and the flowery promises of a beautiful wedding had kept her smiling and unafraid in the nights without him. She ignored the letters the first few days after his death, but then picked them back up. And every night after that first one, she sat in her rocking chair and read the letters.

They grew thin and dirty with the years that passed, and some of the ink faded so much that Nell was simply reading memory. She held the papers in her hand, smelled them as though she might catch whiff of the love she had, and cried into them, layering new tears on top of old. She grew up, but never grew happy.

THE GENERAL STORE TOOK A YEAR to rebuild, really. Or, if it didn't take a year to rebuild, it took a year to rebuild, restock, and regain business. It was a rough year, where Mr. Braunhoff found himself angrier than he had at any point during the war. He thought back to his house arrest, and how unfair it had been. He thought of the haughty attitudes of those that had come into his store and ripped wares from his shelf, preaching that the war was just and good and wouldn't impact them at all, if they just let it roll through on its course.

He was an old man now, and he knew that none of that had been true. He didn't make it to the general store every morning now, offering that to his son and some of the younger men in town, while he and Tillet oversaw the operation. Tillet, too, had become an old man, and often their conversations revolved around the perils of age, and what experience the years had given them. It seemed the young ones were quicker to forget than they were, and it worried them.

He sat on the wide porch of the house he had built for his wife when he first moved to Georgia. He thought back to the days when Will was a baby, and the days when he was a child, running through the mountain with Sam and bringing squirrels to the Lacy. He wondered how much of those days his son looked back on, or if everything in his past was tarnished with the battle. Will had stayed away from the mountain ever since the day he came careening from its forests with eyes that had seen horror and blood.

The house was empty now. His wife had died two years ago, the weight of the war never really leaving her shoulders. Will had left before that to go to the University of Georgia. He had been so happy when his son said he was going on to school—he had assumed Will would stay close to home, never really quite the same as he had been.

Will came back to visit every few months, growing more and more into a man with each passing day. He hadn't married yet, but Mr. Braunhoff was sure he would find a nice woman to settle down with when he was ready. His love was still the railroad. The war hadn't changed that. When he went to school, he decided he wanted to go for engineering so that he might take a position with the railroad in Tennessee.

The letter had come a few months ago saying he was moving from Georgia, to Tennessee, because he had been accepted to work for the Cincinnati Southern Railroad to Chattanooga. It was the first time Will sounded truly excited and not reserved. Mr. Braunhoff took the letter out back the night it arrived, and read it aloud by the grave where his wife lay.

"He's happy," he said, to the air. It felt good to say he was happy. It made him happy, himself.

Sam Tillet had followed his mother's advice, and pursued the seminary instead of a regular education like Will had. Sam had floundered a bit in the days after the battle. Will was distant and hard to reach for years, and their usual pastimes were no longer fun. He eventually stopped trying to force Will to be normal, and started embarking on his own journeys. He appreciated the quiet of the woods, even after the carnage, and took pleasure in watching green sprout and grow over the gashes and trenches in the earth that the ghosts hadn't filled in.

His mother had been happy when he decided to go to seminary, and he realized that he was happy about it too. Seminary was good to him—there was quiet learning, and reflection, and he felt closer to humanity than he had. It was a place to see the good in people, and the world, and it helped heal his own pain around the blood shed at Kennesaw.

While studying one day, Sam felt the immeasurable power of the Lord filling his soul. He felt like he was shaken to his core— that new energy had filled his heart and his soul and he was a vessel of God's love. By morning, he knew what he was meant to do, and started to plan a mission trip to Africa.

The mountain healed, too. It took longer than it did for the people who lived around its base, but it still healed. Trees grew where bigger ones had once stood. Birdsong finally returned to the air, after the smoke and stench faded. Bullets and cannonballs lay where they fell, only occasionally moving with the pulse of the earth as it shifted and the winds blew. Brush grew over them. Dirt covered the bullets. And even the squirrels returned to the hillside, having forgotten what drove them away in the first place.

Epilogue

The day had dawned with the bright sunlight that washed over the trees and land and made people hopeful again. The air was crisp in the hours before the humidity would settle over the land and make it hard to breathe. It was a beautiful day, and there had been hundreds in the years since the last drop of blood was shed on the mountain. It would almost be easy to forget the carnage that had torn the land to bits, except that if you looked closely, that history remained present.

The day wore on and had gotten heavier, both with the heat of the season and the solemn reflection. People prepared for the ceremony that was going to take place, organizing and moving chairs, going over the speeches, and making sure everyone knew where they were going to stand. It had been one hundred and fifty years since the battle of Kennesaw Mountain, and tonight they would take a moment to remember the rampage, and the effect it had on the place they called home.

Later, the local leaders and dignitaries arrived in their conveyances not even dreamed of during the prior conflict, and got out, making their way slowly to the field. They spoke in hushed voices to each other, not wanting to break the quiet peace that had settled once the preparations had been completed. Some of them made their way to the podium and row of white chairs by the monument that stood in silent stone. Others gathered by the rows of chairs for the audience—people who came because they had an interest in the history, or could trace their family back to the Dead Angle themselves. More and more people arrived, carrying with them the memories and sadness that had been passed down through the generations, keeping the boys who had fought on the mountain alive long after they were gone, some making themselves comfortable on blankets where there was no level ground for chairs, reclining where others had lain in lifeless repose.

The general stores and the blacksmith shops and the small cabins were no longer a part of the landscape, but they felt real in the hearts of the people who had come to the mountain to pay their respect. The history of the land was their history, and the battle cries could still be heard in the wind, if one listened closely enough on a quiet night, and opened themselves to the feelings of loss that that the trees still carried in their trunks, growing from the ground that had been fertilized in blood.

The battlefield had changed as trees regrew, and now it was a National Battlefield Park—set aside from the rest of the country to hold remembrance for what occurred there. It was untouched by progress, except for the stone monument that stood there, dedicated to the troops from Illinois that had come and lost their lives so many decades before. Soon the crowd of dignitaries and locals reached the hundreds. They had come to see the rededication of the monument, and soon the speaking would start.

There were speeches from park officials and the local government, calling those in attendance to remember the men that lost their lives, and how important it was to remember what a nation looked like when it was split open and raging. They talked of the blood that poured down the hills, and the trees that had fallen. Members of faith got up and shared words of healing with the group, noting how it important it was to understand the country never fully heals from war, without giving it due remembrance. A church choir sang forth songs, concluding with the spiritual "Going Home," bringing a choking sensation to the throat and tears to the eyes, the lyrics drifting over the scene of dreadful carnage one hundred fifty years earlier.

The sun set farther in the sky and the light shone through the trees, casting stripes of light over the land. One ray hit the stone and marble monument, causing the "ILLINOIS" to shine and sparkle, as if by Divine recognition, catching everyone's attention. So many lives from another state had been lost here, men and boys who had ridden the train with hope, only to find their ultimate sadness. The crowds watched the sun glint and illuminate the words for a moment more before time let it slip away, as it so often did.

Darkness soon rose as the words faded and the audience slowly turned to take in the mountain itself. Fifteen decades before, men and boys had climbed this hill with hope and determination, in the sweltering, bug-infested summer days. They had climbed and clamored and raised their rifles and voices for freedom and their ideals. Now, the hill lay silent. Through the grass, going up the incline, candles were lit. They stood small by themselves, but there were many of them, filling the space that had once been trampled by cannon fire.

Each one flickered softly in the evening, their flames rising and twisting toward the sky, as though reaching for heaven. The audience moved slowly through the rows of light. It looked as though stars had fallen from the sky and come to rest amongst the grass—each one a reminder of a life that had flickered on the mountain years before, before going out. Nobody spoke as they moved, taking in the number of candles and the words that had been shared moments before. Others cautiously made their ways in another direction, down a steep, dark pathway to a lone small grave to assure its eternal occupant he had not been forgotten and pay homage for his ultimate sacrifice.

The wind rushed through the trees, shaking the pine needles and leaves but leaving the candles untouched. A heaviness hung in the air, and some of the people felt goose bumps rise on their skin as the understanding of sheer loss settled into their bones like it had settled into the bones of those who had been left behind. If they listened closely when the wind blew, they could still hear the sound of rifle fire and fallen trees.